WILFRED A

Persephone Book Nº 107
Published by Persephone Books Ltd 2014

First published by Hutchinson in 1976

Endpapers taken from 'Maud', a 1913 furnishing
fabric by Vanessa Bell manufactured in Maromme,
France, in a private collection

Typeset in ITC Baskerville by
Keystroke, Wolverhampton

Printed and bound in Germany by
GGP Media GmbH, Poessneck

9781903155974

Persephone Books Ltd
59 Lamb's Conduit Street
London WC1N 3NB
020 7242 9292

www.persephonebooks.co.uk

WILFRED AND EILEEN

by

JONATHAN SMITH

○ ○ ○ ○ ○ ○

with a new afterword by

THE AUTHOR

PERSEPHONE BOOKS
LONDON

FOR MARJORIE SELDON

AND ANNE STEVENS

CONTENTS

WILFRED AND EILEEN

CHAPTER ONE

CAMBRIDGE 1913

It was all very well, this fun, but Wilfred was tiring of it. He was feeling a little oppressed by the claustrophobic intimacy, the place was too full of clever men; he was glad to be one of them, no doubt about that, but his mind was stretching forward to London. Wasn't Cambridge enough for him in his final hours there? No, it wasn't, he wanted to escape for a few moments and keep himself to himself. Although he could be witty, so little of his character found expression in forced jocularity; it was true he liked wry jokes, he enjoyed seeing people smile as the subtle force of his remarks stole upon them; and, on the whole, he tended to prefer acerbic people to worthy ones, intelligent men to splendid fellows, unreliable friends to dull and faithful ones, integrity wasn't enough, yes, all that. But not too much of this brilliance, this endless defining, defining, defining. One could be articulate to the point of lunacy and Wilfred sometimes feared his friends would arrive at that as they qualified, organised escape clauses and strove – always on guard and light of foot – to be absolutely, scintillatingly accurate in every nuance of perception. One could, quite seriously, go mad. In the final analysis, Wilfred decided, some of his friends could write a book about the glance of a girl or the look in an enemy's eye. But, really, should one bother? The book would express, in all its fascination and difficulty, the state of their own minds and little more.

Nevertheless they would be amused by the menu for the Ball. Wilfred ran up his staircase and entered his room, a room full of teatime self-applause.

'*Consommé Milanaise,*' Wilfred began.

'It's the menu!'

'Wilfred's got the menu!'

'Quiet for the menu!'

Wilfred raised his hand for less noise. He began.

'*Purée de Pois français.*

'*Tranche de Saumon en Mayonnaise.*'

Groans from some, and a chant set up:

'So we've done the colleges and done the Mays
We've lunched seriatim off the same mayonnaise
But before we go our several ways
Let's all join together in a hearty vote of praise.'

Wilfred raised both hands. Silence, feigned awe. He continued.

'*Filets de Sole en Aspic à la Belle Vue.*'

'Poison!'

'*Cailles en Chaud-Froid à l'Égyptienne.*

‘*Côtelettes d'Agneau aux Pois français.*’
‘What about the vegetarians?’
‘*Ballotine de Caneton à la Gelée.*’

Cheers, building into a crescendo, greeted each item of the ‘*Souper de Bal*’.

It had been quite a week, a week of endless recollection and final fling. Wilfred's rooms would in a few months' time be someone else's. Other pictures would be on the wall, a different Pater and Mater on the mantelpiece, another friend on horseback. The basketwork armchair, the central throne of that castle, would belong to some insignificant young fellow. How would Dr Barnes take to the new lot? In a year's time how would Wilfred feel about Trinity?

‘Have you seen *Cheer-oh*, Wilfred?’
‘Yes.’
‘Isn't Jack Hulbert supreme!’
‘And Cuthbertson playing a woman, for the second year!’
‘Who was he this time?’
‘Sylvia, an American heiress.’
‘What a Wusky Woozle!’

Would the next group who used this room as a meeting place sit up to the small hours reading Chesterton and Kipling, Shaw and Belloc? Would there again be evenings in which they read Masefield's *Daffodil Fields* until they lay on the floor laughing at the light imitations of it, when they all thought David Rutland had a seizure and David wasn't sure whether he had or not? Or evenings like it? Probably. Well, certainly. But not *quite* like it. The new men might walk along the Roman road and the pre-Roman dyke. They might tread on the sandwiches and turn over the boat. They would probably do the Devil's Ditch. But walk to Ely and back? Never.

Wilfred and his friends were spending their last, exhausting week at Trinity. Tripos exams were over; depressions, emotional crises and religious doubts, those basilisk hours, were forgotten in extrovert, careless intimacy. Unpleasant people, who had been both an offence to the spirit and an affront to the aesthetic judgment, ceased to irritate. Late-night dinners, morning walks, breakfast parties, straining one's stomach in the rugger boat, dancing with Diana, getting photographs taken of all one's gang, and there were so many, yes, even dreary old Fox. Intellectual vehemence was giving in to the ultimate orgy of temptation and fun; and Wilfred was trying to give in with the best of them.

The menu had given way to teatime thrusts at 'the ridiculous men one met'. Once someone was defined – Punny Piers, for instance, Piers Bentley – he was dead; as the strongest opinions were the most cheered no one dared be tentative, and the more absurd the ridiculous man was the more sublime the joke.

'Wilfred, what about Monte?'

'Monty who?'

'Montenegro!'

Hysterically they remembered the party shortly after the Balkan wars were over when Blandford and Bentley had come in dressed as the King of Montenegro and the Crown Prince of Greece. The uproar had been as lively as it was nasty when

4

Hanky Panky carried them away with her oratory about votes for women.

'Do you know I thought Hoppy Wilkinson was going to pour cocoa on her.'

'Positively squalid!'

'It was nearly Homeric.'

'It *was* Homeric!'

'Do you remember his outburst in the vernacular? I had to stop him.'

'Mrs Pankhurst is a prophet, you told him.'

'Will someone have some pie and tinned fruit?'

'Now, look here, this isn't a night operation and there isn't a war on. Pie and tinned fruit grace a night op, not May Week.'

'Have you heard of the Blackmailing Bedder in Nevile's Court? She found a w blank m blank n in you-know-who's room and told him there were £1 bedders and 10s. bedders and she was a £1 bedder.'

'Bed-her!'

'That's a bit steep.'

'Don't pay. Refuse. Pray for the remission of her sins.'

The door was bounced open and Piers Bentley bounced in with it. He addressed the room:

> 'Would you like to sin
> With Elinor Glyn
> On a tiger skin?
> Or would you prefer
> To err with her
> On some other fur?'

'Fast and improper.'

'A familiar piece of rot!'

A tiny ball of paper was flicked across the room:

'Bentley, write all you know on that!'

'I hate insincerity in any man,' Piers replied, 'except one of high character.'

'When is Diana arriving tonight, Wilfred?'

'What are the girls reported to be wearing this year?'

'According to my sources,' Wilfred replied, 'mauve, or pale rose or lavender.'

'What is Diana wearing this time?'

'Mauve, or pale rose or lavender.'

'Ouch!'

'There *is* gentlemen as *are* gentlemen, Mr Willett, and you ain't one.'

It was all becoming too much for Wilfred.

'Is she peach melba, syrup and a bit too much cream?'

'If she is, Wilfred, I'll swap her for my venison.'

'Is she game?'

'*Is* she!'

'Is she worth the ticket? Did you take her to the Mays?'

> 'The sort of grass they grow at Ditton
> Is classier, but vile to sit on.'

'Oh, do shut up, Piers.'

'To be frank to the point of unseemliness, Wilfred is not too keen. Well, we ask ourselves, why is he taking her tonight? Could it be that Wilfred is perverse?'

'I know, if you're really good, I'll arrange a little dance for you with Mrs . . .'

The sentence died away as Wilfred stood over Piers threatening him with a candlestick and cushion.

'I'll see you lot later,' he said and left his room to his friends.

Wilfred jumped down the wooden stairs, across Great Court, tapping the sundial as he went, never forget to do that, past Hall, under the Wren Library and out through the iron screens on to the Backs. He walked vigorously, a slim, strong, wiry figure, given to sudden changes of direction and pace. When he found his favourite spot on the sloping bank, underneath a willow tree, where he enjoyed the sensation of being slowly but imperceptibly pulled by his heels into the river, he sat down and lit a pipe with quick, deliberate movements. He was tired from the late nights and the tug-o'-war (although slight he was always in the team – the compliment pleased him), and he was tired of the drink. He lay back and closed his hooded grey-blue eyes.

Diana. He could not really explain his changing moods about her, and if he could he certainly wasn't going to try in front of that ribald gathering. He and Diana were genuinely fond of each other and had always been, well, sensible – did being sensible mean one cared more or less? He blew out smoke. She was too polished by the company of charming men, she was so assured. It was a bit of a problem and underneath the banter he was becoming a little apprehensive about the Ball. He was irritated too by Piers but he wasn't exactly unhappy; he could, he was sure, dance all night with six silly girls and still enjoy the sense of belonging to his friends. What did Diana's glances suggest? Was she thinking of someone else? Perhaps Diana did not do much thinking? And there was something about her hands he didn't like, something about the nails. Oh, enough of Diana, it shouldn't go too badly. Soon he'd be at the London Hospital, 'that charitable medical institution', doing a short summer course before starting full time later in the year; it would be back to lectures, no more frolicking. 'Lectures are but a sleep and a forgetting,' some wag was always saying; but for Wilfred they were absorbing. If he wanted to be the greatest surgeon 'that charitable medical institution' had produced – he loved that resonant phrase – he must not miss any chance to be more knowledgeable. It was the largest general hospital in England and no accident or urgent case was ever refused admission. Wasn't that worthwhile, wasn't that magnificent! They had installed Finsen light and elaborate X-ray equipment; they were fighting cancer and venereal disease.

'Hello, Wilfred.'

Oh, no, it was Piers Bentley again, Bentley, a fool to his fingertips, a victim of his own tireless, grasshopper style. Why did he have no judgment or self-control? When he did digress into seriousness he became merely obtuse. Wilfred really could do without him at this moment. It was all so unfair the way virtues and vices were parcelled out, the dull, gay, exciting, boring, the ineffectually clever. Was it simply a matter of good luck to be good, or pleasant or unpleasant?

'Hello, Piers.'

'Are you looking forward to tonight?'

'Yes, rather. Who are you taking?'

'Amanda.'

'Is she nice?'

'Terribly *fin de*. Sorry, Wilfred, that's a crib. Lear, I'm afraid.'

Piers sat next to him on the bank. Wilfred rolled over on to his stomach and looked across the Backs. A much better prospect.

David Rutland and a girl were approaching them from St John's. Wilfred liked David. He liked his friendly, open nature and the ease with which he lived; he seemed supremely tactful and able to move effortlessly through any kind of situation. Everywhere he went David was popular; even his buttered toast somehow tasted better than everyone else's. He managed to talk freely, without sneering or flattery; only he could spend evenings with two or three Fellows without appearing subservient or familiar. So balanced and mature: with some it would have been indecent, but not with David. Looking at him now Wilfred wondered if such people kept their crises private or whether they had none. They seemed groomed for life, tailored to fit. And the girls – this one looked splendid – the stream was unending; indeed, David made a point of dispensing them, as if aware of but not embarrassed by his riches. Wilfred especially admired David's appreciation of music; they had really enjoyed two evenings hearing the Moody-Manners Company perform Gounod's *Faust*. Tapping his pipe out on the grass Wilfred got to his feet and was introduced to the girl; she lived in Kensington, too, a Miss Stenhouse. Wilfred stepped a couple of feet back down the slope and looked at the other three as they chatted. David didn't seem to mind Piers, nor was he obviously humouring him. Miss Stenhouse was taller than most girls, much the same height as Wilfred. She had fine wavy hair and a slim, graceful figure. Her clothes had nothing *outré* about them; but they were pleasingly subtle. She listened attentively to what they were saying. Soon, with a cheery 'Goodbye', the three wandered on their way. Miss Stenhouse and David made a good couple, and Wilfred was happy for them.

Wilfred sat down and looked at the placid curves of the river, reflecting: his earlier life had followed a well-known path and soon he'd be home again with Mater and Pater. His family was only a little bit more than middle class, conventional, affluent and snobbish. School had impinged but not particularly impressed: there had been some valuable work done at St Paul's, a few forgotten boys he had loved, the little extra needed to be done to pass the 'Little-Go' had been done, and he had duly arrived at Trinity. What was worth remembering of his life so far? He settled down again to watch the Cam move, if it could be said to be moving, by.

The photographs in his Great Court room tell as much as need be told. There was one of himself standing outside the school at lunch hour on the last day, linking arms with Rudkin and Armstrong. Boys scurry in the background and the clock stands at two. Then there was Wilfred helping to chair the winner of the King's Prize at Bisley. Wilfred was an excellent shot himself, captaining the best St Paul's team in memory. He had, of course, been to his share of tennis parties, laughing with the girls in the groups at the net. The number of friends who wanted to know who *they* were! And that fish! The one he had caught at Tintagel, the outrageous way he had shown off to Kate Lewis about it. There had been a pleasant holiday or two with Pater and Mater before things had become openly strained. Some other girl came with them to Seal one year, surely. Mater said she had 'too bold an eye'. Yes, there she is in the background but Wilfred couldn't remember her name. At the Military Tournament he took a delighted Mater into the Cambridge OTC enclosure, and later sat with Frost, Howard and Harrowing for the Wale Plate photograph; they stared impassively into the distance as if winning the Wale Plate was just one of those things. Pipe, rod and rifle – they weren't enough to satisfy him – but they had been his way. Well, yes, there was also one romantic shipwreck pose, with his eyes narrowing into the sun – how did he let himself in for that one?

Back home soon, Kensington. Home, there self-control was the unwritten law. Viewed now, looking back, it had been a reasonable life – but the atmosphere was often anxious of doing something 'wrong'. David Rutland was fond of saying that too many of them had been badly brought up in the best tradition. Wilfred nodded silent agreement. Politics and money were discussed at home; religion and literature were not. Religion was taken as read, and literature simply wasn't. There were too many trivial courtesies. There was too much reverence for nothing in particular and not much affection, either expressed or otherwise. When girls were invited to tea Wilfred darkly suspected some mysterious rota system was in operation.

What to make of it all?

'Very run of the mill,' Wilfred murmured to himself, and refilled his pipe. Yes, perhaps, but it had been a training, even if he hadn't been set on fire. It was an experience even if the mill had ground slowly. Although the years seemed in retrospect too like a calm sea with little to lift him up, he felt there was some design taking shape in his medical career. The harder he worked at Cambridge, and he worked hours more each day than nearly all his friends, the more intensely he enjoyed life and seemed to be clearing from his past the clouds of his mother. She had been the proprietor too long, he knew that now, and his father would still be banker when he started at the Hospital. Despite being tied to his family by the allowance, he hoped Hospital would be a new context, a wider passage. In his blood, in his stomach, he felt the steadiness of the past giving ground to an unsure, vigorous future. But, no more thinking – he had to meet Diana.

* * *

A softening nine o'clock light was falling on the gates as the crowd watched the young ladies arrive for the drinks and noisy gatherings before supper. Cars and carriages, feathers and furbelows, hats and chaperons, gowns of floating texture and of white satin – it *had* to be a success. Everyone proclaimed it was going to be and who were the resolute chaperons and fluttering young ones to doubt it. One or two were determined to be entrancingly bored but for Diana, the evening was perfect, quite perfect.

'Isn't everything perfect?' she said to Wilfred, 'isn't it the most wonderful sight?'

Inside the college friends were joining together for hushed plans of hazardous escapades, Wilfred was introducing Diana, dressed in the prettiest pale rose and most enticing lavender, to everyone he cared for, to anyone. The colour and bustle was already quickening his pulse, and the entertainment had not started. Now it had. The Blue Viennese Band was swirling the swathing chiffons and lace; laughing couples sped past Wilfred and Diana, they joined in, and soon all was bewitching music, tilted heads, glancing eyes and gliding feet. Keeping their long vigil the chaperons were suitably placed: with thanks and assurances given every door to civilised abandon seemed open.

'We all know the menu, we do,' they chorused as they settled noisily to supper. Rather shyly Wilfred explained to Diana that he had persuaded the Kitchen Manager, a man of variable moods, to part with a copy of the traditionally secret details of the feast. David Rutland raised his glass to Wilfred.

'To our Wilfred!'

David always made Wilfred feel worthwhile. Wilfred looked down, blushing, and Diana squeezed his hand. 'Wilfred, who painted the portrait of Henry VIII?' He looked up. It dominated the brilliant, candlelit scene. He told her all he knew, and talked even more enthusiastically about the Reynolds on the other wall. Diana looked beautiful, she looked fascinated, but Wilfred noticed her eyes were rather too wide open. Pointless. He settled down to the certain delights of the meal. Why couldn't he hold her attention on the things that mattered, why did he seem to bore her when he was trying to be interesting? He looked at her. The fair hair, and delicately proportioned features were striking in profile; she was a girl to notice in any company, and from the clustering around her in between dances Wilfred knew that he was the envy of the group. Diana turned half away to listen to a remark from David, perhaps a compliment, fairly safe guess, yes a compliment. Diana smiled, radiant with appreciation.

'How's your lamb, Wilfred?' Piers called out, 'mine's delicious.'

'Very good, thank you,' Wilfred replied, refusing the ambiguity.

'I do not joke for my own amusement,' Piers retorted.

Wilfred smiled.

When the clock struck half past ten Wilfred told Diana about the double chiming, only regretting he couldn't exactly remember the lines Wordsworth wrote about the clock.

'Of course, Wordsworth went to St John's.'

'Only mistake he made,' from the other side of the table.

'We can allow them Wordsworth, surely,' David said. 'They're a bit thin on the ground.'

> 'There was a young man from St John's
> Who tried to de-dum the swans. . .'

Stifled sniggers.

'Shall we go for a walk after the dessert, Diana?'

'I'd like to later, Wilfred, but I've promised to dance with David; and Piers. And of course I'm looking forward to those with you. Thank you so much for this marvellous supper.'

14

'It's nothing, really. I must say you are beautifully dressed. That really suits you.'

'How sweet of you, Wilfred. Thank you.'

'I'm sure you'll enjoy seeing the Cloisters and the Gallery. But there's plenty of time, of course.'

If only Wilfred had that manner of David, that confident modesty which girls so admired; he watched them go down to dance. Wilfred was popular with his circle of fellows, but always felt they were more witty, more able, more everything than he. However often he was told this was rot, he genuinely felt it to be true. He expected them to do well in examinations and was surprised when he did.

He could hear the *Valse Septembre* across the college and it seemed to him appropriate that Diana should be dancing with David; he was expecting her to cut him off some time, diplomatically planned, but doubted it would be at the Ball. She had too much style for that, and was, to be fair, too nice.

Wilfred turned to see Miss Stenhouse a few seats away. There was something playful and yet determined about the classical line of Miss Stenhouse's mouth: she was the sort of person to whom it would be fun to give a present. Wilfred was particularly struck by her indifference to being alone for a while; in this situation most girls were rather obviously put out or rather obviously preoccupied with their hands. He caught her eye – the shine was bright, a shine rather than a sparkle. The smile was not helped by any effort or plan; it happened across her face. Her hand lifted involuntarily from the table in acknowledgment, and dropped as the smile faded.

Wilfred felt he would like to talk to her and this was surely a good moment, the moment seemed to matter. Don't hesitate, Wilfred: Wilfred was always looking back at things or ahead to things, never occupying the space – he reprimanded himself for this. But she might take a low view if he obviously moved across to talk to her. Who did he think he was? You couldn't just barge in like that. He was beginning to feel a slight knotting of his stomach. He felt insecure. Perhaps the light-hearted approach was the right one? He'd been good too long and being good wasn't enough. This is silly, don't be so silly about simply talking to a girl. After all, Diana is enjoying herself with . . . no, no. That has absolutely nothing to do with it, don't become one of those people who only does something in reaction to someone else doing something. Wilfred ate a grape and shot a look across the table. Wilfred wanted nothing more from people than they would freely give. And the smile had been generous. It was only fair to talk to her. He asked her if she was engaged for the dance.

'No, indeed I'm not,' and her card was duly marked.

'And might I perhaps claim the next one, too?'

'I'm afraid not. I shall sit that one out.'

'But it's the Pink Lady, one of my favourite tunes. Do you not like it?'

'You can certainly dance the next Two-Step with me, but not the thirteenth dance.'

'You're superstitious!'

'I dare say it's a lot of silly nonsense to you but it's not to me. But perhaps you don't like the Two-Step?'

'Oh, I do. You won't like it if you dance it with me. I'm not the best of dancers, really.'

'I don't mind, but I don't expect it's true.'

'Perhaps I can take you for a walk to give you time to dispel your fears.'

'What fears?'

'That the roof will fall in during the Pink Lady.' She laughed. It was rather more than he deserved.

'Come on, I'll show you the beauties of Trinity. Have you seen the Library?'

'Well, I think I saw it this afternoon when David walked me along the Backs. I didn't think it would be quite like that. It's lovely, isn't it? And I remember he said it was designed by Wren.'

'Yes, he designed it for nothing; I mean he didn't charge the college for his labours. But then we deserve it.' Oh, do relax.

'How wonderful of *him*,' she replied. Was she suggesting his facetiousness was misplaced?

'Are you really interested in seeing round the College?'

'Don't be rude. Of course I am. My mother says it's very obvious when I'm bored.'

'You don't look bored.'

'My mother is always right.'

'She sounds like mine. Do you mean she's pleasantly right or unpleasantly?'

'Pleasantly.'

'Not like mine. Perhaps I can show you how ugly New Court is,' Wilfred ventured, 'after we've danced.'

Miss Stenhouse's large brown eyes flashed a little.

'If it's ugly, surely we needn't bother?'

Wilfred was slightly put out; it was going so well, but he didn't want too many of his remarks too quickly deflated. He moved on rather clumsily:

'I do like your dress. The colours are attractive – and unusual.'

'I'm glad you like the colours; creams and light browns are my favourites. But I'm dreadfully spoilt you know. When I was asked to the Trinity Ball my mother told me I could have anything I liked in the dress line.'

'I've never heard a girl *admit* that kind of thing before. That's splendid.'

'Have you known David long?'

'Ever since we've been at Trinity. Where did you meet him, might I ask?'

'At a concert and then at a party earlier this year.'

'Could I call you by your Christian name? I'm afraid I don't know it.'

'Of course you may. My name is Eileen.'

'How do you do. I'm called Wilfred.'

'I know, I remember from this afternoon.'

'Do tell me more about yourself, your family. Are you a large family?'

'Well, my cousin Rupert says we live "a life of ease and abundance". It sounds both a compliment and a criticism the way he says it, but that may be just because he's intelligent. I'm one of four sisters. Do you really want to know? Well, it's rather complicated. My father died when I was quite young, and my mother then married my stepfather who also was a widower; and he had two daughters from his first marriage. So, you see, I've two older half-sisters, they're both married, and one full sister, Victoria. We're all very different, I think.'

'How interesting. I'm the only child, I'm afraid.'

'Ah, and finally – and then I shan't breathe another word about my family,' she said, 'we're pretty packed out with servants.'

'How packed?'

'Twelve!'

'Nine more than us. You have routed us. But Rose makes up for many. She's what Mater calls "clever with her fingers". Annoying phrase, isn't it?'

'How long have you been at Trinity?'

'Four years, finishing tomorrow. But I'm not going to be sad, there's so much to do, isn't there? This may be the end of the fun but I'm looking forward to going on with medicine.'

'That's a good thing. I'm afraid I often feel I'm leading a rather pointless existence.'

'Do you? Oh, look, I've talked through some of the dances, I'm sorry. Are you ready for this possibly gruesome experience?' Wilfred's heart was hammering as he took her hand; oh, for some of that laconic confidence he showed in the tea parties with his friends. Her hand was long, slender and not unwilling; what was he to say now? Say something.

'I do like your pendant. What is it made of?'

'They're diamonds, and olivines, I think.'

'Olivines? Never heard of them.'

'Nor had I.'

They danced, Wilfred making some whimsical remarks about other couples they moved through, not perhaps his best remarks but growing in edge. Then suddenly:

'Let's walk again, shall we? We could look at the garden of the Lodge. It's illuminated tonight. They say there's nowhere we can't go.'

'Do they? Who's they?'

'Tradition, I suppose.'

'What can't you do normally?' Eileen teased.

'We aren't allowed to smoke in cap and gown. If we're caught we're sent to the Dean and fined. Don't laugh, that's serious.'

With their shadows slanting ahead of them they walked away from the lights along the cloisters. Wilfred occasionally had to guide her elbow up and down the slight bumps in the stone, bumps he knew so well. He did not want her to stub her toe, not now, please.

'Have you read any Byron?' Wilfred asked.

Sounds of laughter came inappropriately from the room above.

'No, I'm afraid not. I'm very ignorant, terribly ignorant. I do read novels.'

Her voice was even more compelling as they walked through the partial darkness; the voice and the strange light made conversation more easy.

'There's a statue of Byron in the Library; the trouble is it's bound to be locked so I can't show it to you now. Westminster Abbey turned it down, you know, because Byron was thought to be immoral. Isn't that funny? If I could produce one work of art, well, one work of any kind, as good as that statue I think I'd die happy.'

'You're making me want to see it. Who made the statue?'

'Thorwaldsen.'

'Never heard of him. Again. How awful.'

'Well, nor had I until this afternoon but I rather wanted to show off. Would you like to see it when the Library opens tomorrow morning?'

'I'm afraid I can't. I have to leave for London at nine-thirty. And don't you think we ought to go back now? I have some dances arranged, and I'm sure you have.'

'Yes. What a pity, but we must.'

They retraced their steps.

CHAPTER TWO

LONDON 1913

Wilfred spent the rest of the Ball with Diana, and most of that time constructing a letter. When he wrote it the next morning he was not satisfied:

> Trinity College
> Cambridge
> June 11th, 1913

My dear Miss Stenhouse,

Forgive a letter so soon after saying 'Goodbye' to you in the half light of the early hours. I wanted to say how much I enjoyed meeting you last night. You can imagine how dreary it is collecting together one's things and preparing to leave Cambridge, everyone seems rather down. The time I spent with you last evening, however, helps to lighten the proceedings.

In a way I would rather not meet many people in the Court and around the College because I would like to slip away now and keep my feelings to myself. I do dislike farewells, don't you? If you are willing I should enjoy calling to see you when I have everything settled at home and when my arrangements at the Hospital are completed. It seems I shall be living part of the time at home and part in the Hospital. Thank you again for the dances and the pleasure of talking to you. Perhaps we will meet in Kensington.

With my best wishes,
Yours sincerely,
Wilfred Willett

It simply wasn't good enough, it didn't strike the right chord; it was lacking in the necessary style and warmth. It might well fail. She had been decent to him and that was all there was to it.

The week that followed at home was both busy and empty. Wilfred felt rather tense and confused as he piled his books into heaps in the corner of his bedroom. It was nice to be fussed again by Rose and to tell her a rather glamorised account of the May Week 'goings-on', and it was with a slightly sick feeling of anticipation that he sorted through his medical notes; but he was drab. With dull eyes and a cheerful voice he expounded to Mater and Pater on the value of being at Cambridge and how it should stand him in good stead with the chiefs at the Hospital. Yes, he was making a fairly convincing case but how did he make a positive move towards her? The letter, so carefully and sensibly phrased, had failed through lack of courage; if he really felt drawn to her, why not write in a natural and unrestrained way? Probably because it had been no more than a walk made possible by a curious set of circumstances – the drink, a strange ethereal light and her superstition.

Wilfred was impressed by much of what he saw in his first days at the Hospital, especially the general efficiency and competence. He became quite friendly with one of the sisters and listened to a few stories about Mr Jenkins and Mr Bowman. How often he heard those names! But as he lay in bed at night his mind dwelt on that mistake, that negligence. On reflection he felt naïve about it but Wilfred had never realised that medical men, even the most famous, make blunders – and that, perhaps worse, they could be petty and political. He was therefore all the more shocked when he thought he detected a gross error with 'Number Five'. Yet a sense of not being sure of his ground in the face of experts and a deep loyalty to the whole idea of the London Hospital kept him from speaking out about the incident; indeed he half blocked his mind. Anyway, to whom could he speak? Possibly the sister, she was friendly. Perhaps it disturbed him so deeply because he came upon the problem so early. The patient was his first surgical dressing.

'Number Five' was a slender young man, fair-haired, and quick-witted. He told Wilfred he was just recently engaged. Because the 'firm' was on full duty he had been operated on for a ruptured appendix by the junior chief; the senior was away on his summer holiday. The patient had been in for three weeks and he knew much more about his dressing than Wilfred did. Every nervous action of Wilfred's was jealously watched and all his mistakes were keenly pointed out; usually in good humour.

After a few days Wilfred's fear of the patient's knowledge changed to concern as his eyes became less aggressive, almost beseeching. The dressing began to stink. He looked directly at Wilfred.

'It's not right, is it?'

Wilfred turned on his heels and went to the Ward Sister: 'Surely Number Five has a faecal fistula?'

She nodded her head but did not look up from her job.

'He's looking more yellow, and I think he's too thin.'

She nodded again.

'Oughtn't it to be closed or drained, or something?'

Sister Forsyth put down her pencil and glanced up at Wilfred. With a quick burst of confidence, she said:

'Of course! But Mr Jenkins can't come in here because they're not his beds. He filled them up while Mr Bowman was on holiday. Mr Bowman just fumes; they're not his cases, he's not interested, and he wants the beds. I've had more deaths this month than the whole year. I'm so worried I feel quite sick.'

Wilfred was shocked. Although he had not yet worked for either of them he had heard about the rivalry and disparaging remarks common between Mr Jenkins and Mr Bowman: the student dressers on the firm knew their different backgrounds, and their contrasting approaches.

'But, Sister, we must do something. Would you please ask Mr Jenkins if he can find a moment for Number Five?'

'He'll bite my head off. You could ask him.'

'Sister, I haven't worked for him yet. You have far more chance of success than I do.'

She sat down again at her desk.

'What sort of man is Mr Jenkins?'

'Very brilliant, driving, hard to please. He is generally considered the most skilful of them all. Very Welsh,' she added as an afterthought.

'How old is he?'

'I should say in his early forties. He often tells us that he paid for his own education, he enjoys that. He can be friendly. He can be terrifying, it all depends, I think, whether he respects you. Still, you'll probably have him soon and then you'll see for yourself.'

'What should we do about Number Five?'

'Let's leave it till tomorrow, shall we?'

The next day the patient was vomiting continuously. Although Wilfred knew a dresser had as much say in treatment as a ward maid – (and rightly so, Wilfred thought, because he felt he knew even less) and even though it was officially nothing to do with him if the man died, he decided to persist.

'Sister, do you remember the Chairman saying the other day that all patients in this Hospital were so well looked after that they were given champagne if the doctor ordered it. Well, it may be useful in the case of regular vomiting. Let's get some for Number Five.'

'All right,' Sister Forsyth said, 'I'll ask Mr Jenkins on his next rounds. You certainly are asking for it. On your own head.'

Wilfred felt he should have done the asking but was glad the Sister would. She told him very firmly to leave it at that.

In a state of emotional excitement Wilfred hurried into the ward as soon as he could the next morning and up to Number Five's bed, confident of at least a nod of recognition. The man would surely realise it was a developing situation. The bed was neat, clean and ready. Sister Forsyth was standing at the next bed, attending to another patient.

'Sister, did you get the champagne?'

'Yes.'

She pointed at a small bottle, a very small one, not the ones of dances and May Week.

'He was too far gone, I'm afraid. He died last night just before I went off duty. Hadn't you better get on with your work? Mr Jenkins wants to show you all a mastoid dressing at ten.'

The unopened quarter-bottle went into the glass-fronted medicine cupboard. Wilfred made a point of looking at it every day. It remained there throughout the months of his training: the gold wrapping became a little tarnished, the firm's name a trifle frayed by constant dusting.

* * *

Wilfred looked as if he was on holiday. He had a letter from her. He had read it five times. Up the steps he bounded, two at a time, and through the door. He felt like talking to Sister Forsyth.

'Ah, Sister, good morning.'

'Just in time, Mr Jenkins wants you.'

'When?'

‹Now, ten minutes. You must have impressed him yesterday. He came in half an hour ago, leant right over my desk as if he owned me and said "Get young Willett to come along, will you? It might be interesting." That means you'd better hurry. The anaesthetist's gone up already. There seems quite a commotion going on. I think it's the important one they've been planning for weeks. Lucky you.'

'Which one is that?'

'Well, if it's the one I've heard of it's a carcinoma.' They hurried up the stairs together.

'What did you do yesterday to catch his eye?'

'I didn't do anything, really. Nothing to mention. But it is good that he asked for me, isn't it?'

Wilfred didn't have time to explain to the Sister the excitement of yesterday. Anyway he was not sure he could. Mr Jenkins was operating on a woman with a pyloric obstruction, with Wilfred at hand. All seemed to be going smoothly, the operation had nearly finished, when her breathing suddenly became shallow, and stopped. The anaesthetist coolly said, 'There's no pulse, the heart is stopping.'

'Quick with that injection,' Mr Jenkins snapped as he felt the heart through the diaphragm and began to squeeze it. 'Two grains,' he said.

Wilfred concentrated intensely, his eye held by the muscle of Mr Jenkins's forearm: contract, relax, contract, relax. He worked away at the flaccid heart with his hand buried in the woman's stomach. The anaesthetist stimulated the patient to breathe by tongue traction; the House Surgeon rhythmically pressed her chest. The low blowing noise of the oxygen escaping the cylinder was unbearably loud. Before two minutes had passed on the theatre clock, her heart began to work again. The woman, Mr Jenkins said as he left, was not, of course, to be told what had happened.

Was today going to be as dramatic? Could this man ever go wrong?

'Well, good luck,' said Sister Forsyth. Wilfred went into the ante-room.

'Ah, Willett, here you are then. Thought you were going to be late but you're just on time. Please don't be late for me, ever.'

Mr Jenkins was animated. He looked even thinner.

'We have a woman coming up with carcinoma of the oesophagus. You're to help me. You want to, don't you? There are plenty of others if you don't.'

'Yes, sir, thank you.'

'Good man. I've decided on excision. Now you're probably wondering – or rather you should be – is he going to use interspinous stovaine?'

Fortunately Wilfred had heard of this controversial method: Mr Bowman was its leading advocate and it was in wide use among the younger surgeons.

'Well, I'm not. Newfangled nonsense. It puts the patients through totally unnecessary nervous strain. You don't approve of that, now, do you?'

'No, of course not.'

'Quite. Anyway, it's far more dangerous than the risk of a little cough or sickness from an ether inhalation.'

'And that can happen?' Wilfred asked.

'If it's badly administered, yes. But, Willett, what these fools don't realise are the dangers of their new technique. Do you know the patient can see everything, every damn thing, except the operation of course. The patient can hear every word, imagine it, you know how loose-tongued some people are. And the patient can often feel himself actually losing strength. I've seen them go white and pant with shock, I'm not exaggerating, with a frightened look in their eyes, like, like a tame animal submitting to you for a beating. Like an animal that doesn't know why it should be hurt. I'd never go through that, if I had the choice, would you? And some of these poor devils don't have any choice.'

Wilfred was glad he did not have to see it used.

'Besides, Willett, getting the needle between the vertebrae to inject the fluid is extremely difficult. I know, I've tried. Once I made a patient shriek with pain. At all events, today, in this operation it cannot be used. Oesophagus. Anything above the waistline is out. Now I've been looking for a way around the problems in this case. It's taken weeks. I knew what I needed, but couldn't see the way to it: anaesthesia with breathing inhibited. I asked Mr Clough – have you met Mr Willett, Mr Clough – no? – well, I asked Mr Clough for his advice. I asked Mr Clough because, of course, he is our best anaesthetist. He has been working very hard for the last fortnight and has now invented the apparatus we need. And I'm delighted with it.'

Mr Clough looked pleased and took up the explanation.

'The result is intratracheal administration of oxygen and ether, with just enough pressure to do away with the need for the patient to breathe at all.'

'Brilliant, isn't it?' said Mr Jenkins. 'If we succeed it'll cause a tremendous stir.'

'Could I ask a question, sir?'

'Of course. Always ask.'

'Does the patient know the risks? I mean has she consented to the operation knowing exactly what's going to happen?'

'Yes. Well, I haven't been able to explain it in technical terms as the woman would not have fully understood. But I've talked to her about it. She agrees to it.'

Wilfred suspected Mr Jenkins's persuasive words, his Welshness. He admired it.

The patient, bright with hope, was wheeled in on the trolley to the ante-room adjoining the theatre. Wilfred helped to put her on the table. Mr Clough inserted a tube into the trachea. Could the woman survive the operation? The sound of her breathing subsided, it was too risky, Wilfred was convinced it was. Her chest was still, although her colour remained good. He watched intently as Mr Jenkins started neatly and carefully. He was immensely careful, not at all as he was with easy operations – Wilfred had heard from other students that he sometimes slashed and slashed and then used his extraordinary skill to get the patient through despite the shocks. Even yesterday Mr Jenkins let blood throb out of a big vessel, let it throb out deliberately while he turned to Wilfred and said:

'Never be frightened of haemorrhage during an operation. It can easily be controlled if you keep your head. Watch this.'

Then he dexterously ligatured the vessel.

But this time there was no demonstration. Mr Jenkins was learning; perhaps success would give him fame, Wilfred sensed Mr Jenkins understood the risks, he wanted them and understood them. Wilfred was drawn into the isolation of a mind at full stretch, living only for the moment.

Carefully, Mr Jenkins excised the angular growth. He brought the free ends together. After an hour, Wilfred cut the gut from the needle to complete the last stitch. The patient seemed to have withstood the operation extremely well.

'Thank you, Willett, we'll see how things go. You did well.'

The next morning, Wilfred went in the moment dressers were allowed to visit the women's ward. The patient was alive, awake. She told Wilfred she was comfortable and smiled at him. Her pulse was not too weak, considering, and Wilfred felt there might be some hope. The following day there was none: pneumonia set in and she died in the evening.

'We've failed, Willett,' Mr Jenkins said, 'but it was worthwhile. Others will benefit from that work we did, mark my words. Never give up, Willett, some give up far too easily.'

Wilfred was depressed. As he left the hospital for home his hand moved to his pocket and he took comfort in her letter:

10 Ashburn Place, SW
June 26th, 1913

Dear Mr Willett,

How kind of you to write to me. It was an unexpected pleasure to meet you at the Ball and very interesting to be shown round Trinity in such an entertaining way. I am used to people thinking I would not be concerned with buildings, history and so on, and all the more grateful to you for treating me to that walk.

My mother and sister are bothering me for what you might call a valse by valse, course by course, story of the Ball but I agree with you. I prefer sometimes to keep my feelings and thoughts all to myself. Although this has made me very unpopular, I am resolute.

If you would care to call I should, of course, be pleased to see you. Good luck for your time at the London Hospital.

Yours sincerely,
Eileen Stenhouse

He, too, would leave it a week or so; in a few weeks, in early July, perhaps, he would telephone her and casually fall into how things were going along.

The next day he was put through to that number he knew so well but he had never asked her for. He had a brief word with Mrs Stenhouse, fencing with her and sensing a slight implication about the rightness of this communication; and then a few more words with another Miss Stenhouse who had curiously thought the call might be for her. A pause.

'Hullo.'

'Hullo, Miss Stenhouse? Miss Eileen Stenhouse?'

'Yes, it is. Hullo, how are you?'

'Better now that I've got through to you. I don't mind saying I nearly gave up – do all of you line up when the telephone goes?'

'I don't think so. But strange gentlemen are different.'

'They sounded pretty formidable.'

'Isn't that another word for large?'

'I'm sorry, is it? I certainly didn't mean that. And they aren't?'

'Certainly not!'

Wilfred blurted it out:

'When can I see you?'

'I'm not sure. What do you have in mind exactly?'

'I mean I know you must be busy.'

'The one thing I am not is busy.'

'Well, on Tuesday afternoon I'm going to see an exhibition of some of my favourite artists. Do come with me if you'd like to.'

'I'd like that very much.'

'You mean you don't have to go away and ask? It may not be suitable.'

'I'd like to very much. Thank you.'

'May I call at two then?'

'That would be fine.'

And goodbyes. It was short, but enough. Closing the door in the drawing-room Eileen cleared up the inevitable questions from the watchdogs as briefly as she properly could, employing the useful evidence that he had been one of the charming men she had been introduced to at Trinity; in no sense, however, did that satisfy their proprietary tone.

* * *

'Do you like that one?' Eileen asked, pointing at a sharp, arresting picture.

34

'Not much, do you?'

'Yes, I'm not sure why and I don't think I can explain it. I like looking at it but I don't know what it means. Do you think it *has* to mean something?' Eileen's face, pale olive and natural in its curiosity, turned intently on Wilfred. It was fun answering his questions; they weren't silly, and she was enjoying this visit as much as the last one.

'Well, if I like something,' Wilfred said, 'and I can't explain why or what it means I say it doesn't have to mean anything but it's still good. If I don't like something and don't know what it means I say it is bad and should mean something.'

They laughed and moved on to the next, sauntering and commenting.

'That's what I'm like with people,' Eileen said. 'I often don't know why I like them, I either do or I don't. If I don't like them, however good they are, and they often are good, I don't care about them. If I like them I'll do anything for them, and no one had better attack them.'

'Do you hate really charming people as much as I do?' Wilfred asked. 'The pictures I like best are the ones that say "I don't care whether you like me or not." All the pictures in our house have been chosen because they fit the room. Rather like the dresses my mother wears; but it shouldn't be like that, should it?'

'It has to come into it. You can't choose pictures that clash with everything else.'

'Oh, yes, it has to come into it. But it's a minor point. Most of the best pictures here unsettle me. I stare at them and wonder what they're all about later on when I get home.'

While browsing through *The Times* Wilfred had come across this exhibition of modern art, and it was proving a good choice for his second London meeting with Eileen. By having objects to discuss and admire he avoided the problems of shyness, of eye contact and wondering what to do with his hands. He could talk to her without appearing too keen and without seeming too vulnerable; she too was glad of the catalogue without realising the motive of Wilfred's choice. Once more she was delighted that he should think her worth this kind of intellectual challenge. So many of her friends went to Goodwood or feeble plays. Eileen looked at Wilfred as he shuffled sideways through some hovering people: he was very upright, rather tense, and carefully groomed with a knotted silk tie. He seemed altogether less young than he had been at Trinity although it was barely a month since then. She asked him about the Hospital but he did not say much. His face was London pale, pale from indoors and study.

'Do you like the theatre, Eileen?'

'Yes, sometimes. We don't go often. I much prefer the Ballet. Oh, we did go to see *The Great Adventure* by Arnold Bennett. Granville Barker was in it, that's why we heard of it, I think.'

'I've never been to the Ballet. Would you go with me and explain it all? I'll take your advice as the best available.'

'Of course, if we can arrange it. My mother and sister will insist on coming, but it would be great fun.'

'It's all Russian, isn't it?'

What a sensitive person he was; she was warmed by his tentative approach, his gentle way. He was so without bluster and excessive courtesy, those two features of most young men she met. She would like to talk about the Ballet to him and promised to look into what was available.

'Will you promise me one thing in return, Wilfred?'

'Yes.'

'Don't work too hard. You're looking a bit peaky.'

'I promise. Mustn't look peaky obviously. You look very nice, so you must clearly continue as you are.'

* * *

Mr Bowman could not have been more different from Mr Jenkins. He was a short, stout little man with an aggressive brown beard. Wilfred wondered how on earth he had reached his position. He had a reputation of saying unkind things to the patients and if in the wrong mood he was incompetent. It was even rumoured he had severed a spermatic cord from carelessness. Wilfred assumed people were too frightened to protest. He operated, however, with a relish as if his life – and not the patient's – was at stake. If there were fresh students come to watch him operate – and Wilfred looked very fresh – he stopped in the middle and said:

'The surgeon's most important instruments are his fingers' – here he held up an ungloved hand wet with blood – 'they must be as keen and sensitive as his knife. To use gloves is sacrificing skill to fashion. Your patient's life depends on your skill, not on your adherence to fads. No patient ever took harm from clean hands.'

His eyes sparkled as they moved around the rather frightened group of students seated on the wooden benches in the

old theatre. Wilfred looked down. Mr Bowman turned again
to the patient, thrusting his beard into the wound. Wilfred
was distressed at the lack of gloves, at the dirty red gown.
'Details, details,' Mr Jenkins said. Surely suppuration would
follow these operations? The use of his fingers must have
given Mr Bowman more than usual pleasure. He clearly preferred them to a surgical instrument.

'The little finger is the exact size for dilating the woman's
urethra,' he said, holding it up before worming it into the
unconscious woman.

'Use your fingers to separate the sac,' and he then demon-
strated as if skinning a rabbit.

But although disgusted by Mr Bowman Wilfred's brain was
becoming increasingly cool. He studied everything, good and
bad, at the Hospital. Every day he found new material to read.
He was learning to absorb complex theories and experiments:
it amused him to think that this might have staggered his
masters in the Science Sixth at school, even impressed
his supervisor at Trinity. And when he watched Mr Jenkins in
the theatre part of him remained solitary. 'This is you,' it said,
'you can do this. You must.'

An unspoken bond between Wilfred and Mr Jenkins was
established in those few weeks; they were both experimenting,
adventuring spirits. In Wilfred's mind the possibilities were
becoming unlimited; to Mr Jenkins nothing was inoperable.
Although they rarely spoke to each other – the early con-
versational intimacy proved unusual – the ties were held in
the absorption of work. Like well-trained actors they relied
absolutely on each other's gestures and movements: Wilfred

the servant, susceptible to hints, Mr Jenkins the original, creative performer. To play second to Mr Jenkins satisfied him.

Although Wilfred was beginning to make some casual friendships and was generally admired by the students for his efficiency and 'promise' he made no close contacts. The ragging about not going out for 'too much' to drink, about being Mr Jenkins's 'rising star', about not 'having' nurses came and went: he simply wanted to be a great surgeon and to achieve it he would risk self-immolation. He wanted it, he wanted it for himself, and he would watch every brilliant and mundane thing, yes, Mr Bowman too, he would make not one tactical or professional error.

Generally, Wilfred was quite impressed by the politeness of the chiefs to the poor patients. They were conscious of their power but restrained in exercising it: their suavity and expertise exactly fitted Wilfred's conception, the popular conception, of a Harley Street specialist. Some seemed to have stepped out of pictures he had seen in the Royal Academy. The behaviour of the housemen was in striking contrast. They infuriated Wilfred. They enjoyed keeping patients waiting, even when called in an urgent way by a Sister – sometimes they would go on reading a magazine for ten minutes.

Wilfred, like every dresser, had several spells of duty in the receiving room. All patients passed through there, and Wilfred saw much which was not in keeping with his notion of a doctor's humanity. He had already lost in a few weeks many of the romantic notions he had when he first walked into the hospital, but he could not see why such grotesque behaviour was allowed. It was on the tip of his tongue to mention it to Mr Jenkins; but he had once heard him say 'Don't let's criticise others, Willett, when there's a chance we'll make a ghastly mistake.' Some patients were treated as hopeless inferiors who had come to hospital to get out of work, or, absurdly, to have a bath. The dirty clothes, the smell and the fleas were, he was told, their fault. They were liars and impertinent. And yet they seemed to him deeply miserable and frightened, full of a deep faith in the young doctors who treated them so scornfully.

In the receiving room – treating each case with intense perfectionism – Wilfred was allowed to stitch up cuts, to paint abrasions with iodine before bandaging, to help with diagnosis. Here Wilfred made his first attempt to pull a tooth.

One morning a young man came in determined to have out an aching tooth.

'Take him into that room, Willett, and take it out. The Sister will give you the forceps.'

Wilfred was too frightened to confess his ignorance. The only thing he knew was that the lower jaw can be fractured by unskilful extraction. Unskilful he was. The job was not made easier by the case full of dental forceps.

The patient opened his mouth and touched one of his lower molars.

'That's the one, Doctor, given me hell it has.' He smiled at Wilfred in absolute confidence.

'We'll soon have it out, I think,' Wilfred said as he opened the box. He had never dreamt that there were so many forceps, expecting to choose between a small, medium or large pair. As he had been given gas himself at the dentist he had never seen an extraction. And the forceps – there were blunt, sharp, angled and curved ones – all with different grips: bewildered but trying to give an air of knowledgeable deliberation he picked up several and finally chose a pair which seemed to give him a good grip.

'That one?' he said, tapping a tooth.

The man nodded him to get on with it.

Wilfred got hold of the jaw with his left hand, praying to God that he would not break it, and started pulling. As he did so he felt as if he were lifting a heavy weight off the ground. With a snap the forceps slipped off the tooth.

'Haven't quite got it,' Wilfred said, wondering if he had given the man further hell, 'this looks a tough one.'

'Have another go, Doc. Don't be frightened.'

'We'll try a stouter pair.'

He gripped and pulled as hard as he could. The man's broad shoulders did not move, his thighs bulging with muscles. Nothing happened.

'Sorry,' Wilfred said, 'must be an impacted root. We don't want to break your jaw, do we?'

'That's all right. Have another go.'

The man looked rather hurt when Wilfred said he would get a more 'experienced' man to try.

'Sorry it's so tough, Doctor.'

Wilfred would like to have shaken hands with the man. He was immensely grateful for his patience and confidence, although it was based, like Wilfred's performance, on ignorance. Wilfred sheepishly left the room and confessed that he'd failed. He was immediately called to the theatre 'for dressers' to Mr Bowman and had to go, asking for the man to be dealt with as soon as possible.

Three hours later he asked the houseman how the tooth came out.

'What tooth?' asked the houseman and went on talking to the Sister.

In the evenings, a few thin factory and shop girls would come in. As most women do before going to the doctor they dressed in their more attractive clothes, although the clothes were flashy and cheap. Wilfred sensed they were frightened of pregnancy, yet complaining of sickness, never their fear. Sometimes they came only with aches or pains which they had persuaded themselves were serious. During Wilfred's second spell there, a houseman cut short a girl in the middle of her explanation:

'Get out. Come back on Monday if it still hurts.' He saw Wilfred's surprised look and added after she had gone, 'She just came to be felt.'

'Yes,' said Wilfred, trembling with disgust, 'and you probably didn't do it very well.'

* * *

To avoid the monotony of her fussy sister and lax mother, Eileen tried occupying her mind with a book or a bustling walk, striding out as if there was a tremendous hurry when there was none. He was unusually tactful with her, she liked that. He did not overuse his charm, he treated her with a winning lack of deference, he seemed to have a power which he preferred not to display. She found it difficult to put it more precisely than that: the man had a kind of harmony. He was shy but not gawky, sensitive without being effeminate, easily amused and yet with an evasive smile. Despite very strong views he never dominated her, always looking for an opportunity to draw her out. Strangely, he did not want to talk about the Hospital, but after the daily drabness of her home when topics were so overstressed that eventually they died of their own too much, the conversations with Wilfred were such fun. Would their next meeting be as amusing? Now what exactly did he say when they last parted? She became rather hot because she could not recall the tone he used. He was certainly more exciting to be with than David Rutland. Back in her room she wandered among the furniture, running her finger along the object which happened to be in her line of sight. If nothing else came to hand she lifted the flowers out to drop the dead ones in the wastepaper basket, the remainder back in the vase. A kind of pain sometimes developed in the silence. She disliked this vacant, pointless state, this unpractical vagueness, and each day she felt an increase in the intensity of her moods. When others tried to pry she hid her eyes so that no one could look in. But she felt important, in a private spell.

Agitated by the rain, Eileen ran up the steps to the Gallery. She started when she saw Wilfred.

'You're late,' he said, his eyes quick and coercive.

'I'm sorry, I was caught in the rain. Have you been waiting long?'

'Not long. Well, let's look at some pictures, shall we? I've got to be back soon. Mr Jenkins is putting the pressure on me.'

He led off into the almost empty gallery. The landscapes looked too familiar, the new works seemed silly and Wilfred hurried petulantly on.

'Eileen, I'm sorry about that.'

The gallery was quiet. Although confused by his loss of self-possession she kept her voice firm and poised.

'It's all right, but please don't speak to me like that. I don't like it and you didn't even ask me why . . .' He felt hot and childish, she was conscious of her tone. Neither could build anything there.

'I'm afraid I have to go. I'll be in touch soon. Goodbye.'

They had only been together five minutes, and she did not speak when they parted. He had been very unfair, he should realise that.

That evening, upright in her chair, she felt herself wanting to write things down. She brooded and struggled with her thoughts: what extraordinary behaviour, did he want to be a surgeon so much that he couldn't spend half an hour with her? Had she read too soon the signs of possible attachment? She wasn't going to be treated like that again, like a doormat; obviously he was overworked, obviously he was annoyed that he had been rude – she noticed distress in his face and she certainly did not want studied politeness from him – but whatever the upshot she was not going to be used.

Outside the rain continued to fall. Eileen began mechanically undressing for bed, thinking how varied had been the few hours she had spent with him. Her shadow flitted across the room. She should have been more definite. Throughout she had been too agreeable – even if she felt agreeable she should seem less so. In the future she would not trust her instincts so much – and yet how she hated that kind of thinking.

She tried to feel unconcerned, she tried to tie up her mind. But it strayed.

In the evenings Wilfred often wanted to be left alone. He did not know what to feel. He felt spent. He found himself without the necessary energy even to contact Eileen, although he should, and he was unwilling to pretend. He stayed late at the Hospital, smarting in the Library over his work, or thinking of the housemen or Mr Bowman; sometimes he went for long walks around the darkening streets of the East End trying to arrange his theories into some kind of coherent shape. Was the secret of happiness, as he had often heard, the limiting of one's aspirations, accepting the ordinary scenes of life without any reaching out? That was how his family reasoned and he could see its strength as an argument. Or should he follow his passions, changing his mind and direction as the developing forces, carefree, exciting and surprising, drew him off? The crisp voice of common sense usually won these long debates and yet he often heard those other low mutterings that would not go away. A vague apprehension clung to him. He did not want to analyse his feelings too closely in case they died; some precious flowers should not be picked. Perhaps love came quietly? But he could not leave his thoughts alone and they would not leave him. The desire to see her again was uncontrollable.

He sent her a message, apologising for his behaviour. 'It was unforgivable. That fool who met you the other day has gone. Could you possibly see me on Thursday, at three in the after-noon, wherever you like? I do not deserve this but please reply.'

Although still confused Eileen was beginning to feel the lack of him.

When they met the sentences did not come easily. They walked briskly along and Wilfred looked straight ahead.

'One must choose,' he soon found himself saying, 'the most important thing is to know what one wants. That's what made my schooldays a bit flat. I didn't know.'

'And you do now?' asked Eileen. She found this stiff, formal tone oddly appealing.

'Yes, I'm sure. Well, I'm usually sure but I do have moments when there are obstacles in the way or I can't see the wood for the trees. Then I make a fool of myself. And sometimes I get so annoyed with some of them at the Hospital that I vow never to be like them. They really do behave like demigods, driven by their own vanity. And they seem to think I want to be like that! But Mr Jenkins is different. He's dangerous and good.'

'Tell me about him. You mentioned him last time.'

Last time painfully crossed Wilfred's face.

'It might take quite a while. In fact he's not an easy man to describe.'

They walked on past the Embankment gardens, Wilfred talking and Eileen's eyes slightly downcast. He was happy. She could imagine him depressed, too, but not for long. She wanted him to go on talking in this lively way, for hours – it was such a contrast to her mother and sister always being down on some poor lady. But she must not keep him from his work, she had no right to do that. As she glanced at him a dark cloud of possession passed over her. No, she must not think of him like that.

Wilfred stopped at a flower-seller's, studied the alternatives very carefully and handed Eileen a small bunch. A petal fell on her gloves. He brushed it away and took her hand.

'Thank you so much. I do love flowers. We've some beautiful roses at home, and honeysuckle.'

'I've always liked flowers, too. At school I was very interested in nature, birds, flowers, trees. Rather a pity that I let it slip at Trinity. And walking in the country, I've walked for countless miles.'

He would like to take her for a walk, out of London – they could go by train for a Sunday afternoon – but he'd better not ask, not yet, it would be difficult to arrange with her parents and he had not even called on them. Wilfred said he ought to do that soon.

'You'll always find us in! We spend so much time indoors, even on beautiful days. It is terribly tedious. I read in a novel that there are a thousand ways of being dull. I think we know most of them!'

Wilfred laughed. Why did she enjoy stinging her family with remarks like that – was she simply protecting herself? But she sensed he respected her today. She did not wish to retrace her steps; neither did she wish to rush on.

'You're models of discretion, are you? But you mustn't have a low opinion of yourself. Anyway, you'd soon get fed up with the silly jokes at the Hospital.'

The noise and bustle of this meeting helped Eileen to control her reactions. There was reconciliation in his voice and she needed more meetings like this one.

It was so good now to hold her hand, he felt strengthened by her; he enjoyed her natural way of speaking and the relaxed grace of her walk. There was more to life than the theatre at the Hospital, he didn't want to spoil this.

'It's been a marvellous walk, thank you.'

'Yes, I expect you must go,' Eileen said with a trace of mockery, her hand trailing his. Wilfred glanced round in a conspiratorial way.

'I expect Mr Jenkins is after me already.'

Their eyes met without evasion. She half ran home. That evening she sat in the solitude of her room, softening, a girl again.

Wasn't it strange how easy he found it to talk to her? He was astonished and relieved: she was approachable. With many girls he was either brisk or effusive, either adoring or hating everything; in fact being fashionable. Now he felt strangely warm. He *would* see her again, soon; it was more interesting than the alternative offered by the other students. He had heard enough of their frank revelations, each 'confession' polished like a trophy. Once, when he was especially tired, some fool had asked him if he'd been 'climbing the drain-pipes'. He never wanted to talk of Eileen like that, he would never be 'between you and me' about her to anyone. Those frail, delicate eyelids! When he went home he sat at his desk engrossed in a textbook or staring ahead in a way which made Rose shake her head and Mater raise an eyebrow: what was the dear boy up to, but didn't all men work? Wilfred glanced at her with furtive petulance, struggling for composure. His long fingers gripped his pipe as his brain raced. Surely his thoughts, the energy in his mind, sufficiently excited him without bringing women into things; they only complicated matters and might well deflect his energies. Wasn't it as thrilling to watch Mr Jenkins operating as it was to hold hands, or to kiss her, even to touch her breasts – when it came to that?

His obsession with work meant he was sometimes garrulous when he went for short walks with Eileen; worse, he somewhat ruined an evening at the Ballet by transparent exhaustion. On these occasions he did not even realise she was making allowances and tolerating his fluctuating moods. After she had left him he would try to analyse his feelings but find only his mind spinning through an inextricable whirl of intimate moments, of tenderness, of stifling rooms and burning lights, of imagined passion; later he would wake and find the light still on. Eileen. Did he love her? How could she love him when he behaved like that? Eileen and Hospital, love and work, work and love; he loved, yes, he loved and worked for both. Many of his fellow students treated girls as if they were ornaments or embellishments. In the blue of the morning after their parties they were indifferent to the nurses they had been with. Did they make love to them and no longer feel interested? Did they make love and feel ashamed? Did they not make love and feel ashamed because they pretended? Did they do something in between and feel defrauded, tortured emotions? How did they manage, as they seemed to do, to keep love and work in separate compartments? Wasn't that precisely what he was trying to do? Flesh of one kind, flesh of another; no! No, that was not fair, he was trying to keep things pure, of their essence. His feelings for Eileen were not animal or sacred or mock; he needed to see more of her, he certainly loved her vivacity, and he sensed he was going to find himself in her. Wasn't that love – a reflection back of self? Perhaps. The next few weeks would tell; he planned to see her whenever he could. He was beginning to realise the kind of person he was before he met her and did not like the knowledge. Did that mean he liked his new self?

* * *

One warm night in August Wilfred was irritated to be called to the maternity wards. He was hoping for a couple of hours reading and possibly to write a letter, a well-judged one, to apologise again for the Ballet and to follow up his most recent meeting with Eileen. He hurried along the corridor and met Sister Forsyth. Mr Jenkins, damn him, had suggested Willett should observe the latest admission. Wilfred was given the background of the case; a sixteen-year-old girl had been brought in three hours ago in the first stage of labour.

'Have you ever seen a child delivered?' Sister Forsyth asked.

'No, I haven't even seen a woman in labour,' Wilfred replied. 'Is there anything wrong?'

'Not really, but she is in a terrible mental state. Frankly I doubt whether she is "all there". She's not married and so far we can't trace her mother, and there seems little hope of finding the baby's father. The girl is very small and may be in for a tricky time.'

'How long has she been in labour?'

'Four hours now. She's so undernourished, so feeble and thin as you'll see, that we don't think she'll be able to take too much strain in the delivery.'

Wilfred went in. The room was starkly lit and the girl a hopeless face. He sat beside her, felt her pulse, then watched a contraction, and checked her blood pressure. Her fragile face was blue around the mouth and her eyes brown and striking.

A nurse moved regularly in and out of the ward to see how things were developing, lifting the sheet which lay across the girl's stomach to check the padding. Possibly every four or five minutes, and often when the nurse was out, the girl experienced powerful contractions. She moaned with pain, pulling her shuddering legs up under her swollen, immense lump, squirmed over on to her side, punching the air with one tight little fist and scrabbling with the other to rub the bottom of her spine. Wilfred managed to watch, gradually overcoming his distaste, forcing himself into a frame of detached enquiry: he would not look away! Within a minute the contraction died down and she lay, momentarily flushed and damp with sweat, half asleep with her mouth open, conscious that it was only a brief respite. Two minutes, one minute, and it was repeated: stillness, stirring, squirming, grasping, punching and fading away to exhaustion. Wilfred was beginning to feel ill with incompetence.

'You needn't stay,' the Sister said.

'I'd like to stay. I want to help.'

'I'm afraid there's not much you can do.'

'I'd still like to stay. I feel I'm learning what to do.'

'Of course.'

'How long does it last?'

'Impossible to say, anything up to twenty-four hours but I doubt whether we'd let it go on so long in this case.'

Every few minutes Wilfred checked the clock; amazingly he had been there only one hour, and he already felt a growing bond between himself, the patient and nurse. In slack periods he talked cheerfully to the nurse or whispered encouragement to the girl. Lectures were never as exciting. On two occasions doctors popped in to suggest Wilfred got some sleep and he found it hard to keep irritation out of his polite refusal. By three in the morning he felt he had spent his life in that room; he knew every instrument and its exact place, the syringes, bowls, towels, the distance to the sink, the correct pressure for the required warmth of water. He knew so many details of the girl's body, places he had never seen before, places his feelings sought but mind recoiled from. And now he had seen everything in clear white light, in a kind of intrusion on a girl he had never met or really spoken to; but he did not feel clinical about it. He felt he knew her and cared for her. He stood up to move to the sink; she grabbed his arm.

'Don't go, don't go.'

His revulsion at the internal checks had now lessened and he realised he was intensely involved. He felt heavy in his limbs but light in mind, and anyway what were his feelings compared with hers?

'Stop it, stop it, can't take no more, stop it!'

Wilfred bent over her crying face, holding her wrist firmly, and said, 'Yes you can. You must. Just try to relax.'

But as he spoke that word he knew it was a wicked word, how could she relax, how could she not worry, how dare he talk such nonsense in the face of such pain? Surely it was not necessary, all this, there must be a way around it in the future? But she laboured on and at five o'clock, after a final hour of struggle and pushing, of haemorrhage and torn tissues, the girl gave birth to a girl: the raw knot of life, followed by the afterbirth and stitching. It seemed they would both live.

'I've known far worse ones than that,' Sister Forsyth said, and handed Wilfred and the girl a cup of tea. She drank it and vomited on to the soiled sheet.

'They always do that,' the Sister said cheerfully.

Wilfred climbed the two flights of stairs to the students' rooms. He passed one or two bustling, unconcerned faces, those of the night nurses. He slept for the two hours left to him before lectures and Mr Bowman.

* * *

Most Sunday afternoons in the autumn Wilfred called for Eileen. They had a few weeks to enjoy themselves now that Wilfred's summer course was over – before he began there on full-time studies. They went for a short bus or train ride into the country to walk by the field paths and streams. The public transport was hot and sticky and they ran from the train, their laughter flying through the trees. They were expectantly happy, stealthily happy, along with Saffron and Jooey: Saffron, Wilfred's spaniel bitch and Jooey, the Pekinese Eileen had been given by Wilfred, despite great opposition from her home. After they had walked for half an hour Wilfred suggested a spot to sit and spread his hands to ask if she agreed. Off the dogs trotted, a determined gun dog and a delicate puppy trying to keep up; they began to dart over slopes, around pools and surged through the long grass in raptures. Later, and a little too punctually, they nestled back into the ferns where Wilfred and Eileen were. Wilfred was quickly on his feet, yawning, eyes shy and movements bashful. Three feet from Eileen he felt tentative; holding her he was in control.

The four set off again, languid yet bound by those unspoken promises in the grass. After ten minutes of holding and ambling, Eileen said awkwardly: 'Wilfred, I don't like to bring this up but my parents feel that as you're calling for me so often we should either do something or break it off for a while. I'm afraid they think we should probably stop because you've got such a long career as a student ahead of you. Well, that's their view.'

'If they mean get married by "do something about it" you know I want to marry you. But we've got to wait.' He felt irritable and shamed.

'Wilfred, my people are very nice about you on the whole but they can't understand why I see so much of you without being engaged.'

'You know perfectly well they probably disapprove of me. I know they think you could do much better than me and I'm sure by their standards you could. I'm not going to earn much money for an age, I know that, and it does rankle a bit. But I need my allowance from my father. I can't possibly complete my training without it and you know what a shindy there'll be if I tell my parents we're getting engaged: I really couldn't face it. It would ruin everything.'

His voice was becoming public, even the dogs looked over their shoulders. Pride flashed in him.

'Why can't your people,' he went on, 'leave us alone as we are? We're not harming anyone. And your mother dares to say "I make a rule of never interfering." Huh! I'll do well if they'll give me time and they might even be proud of their daughter's choice.'

'I'm sorry. Don't be rude about them, please.'

Marriage as an intimate union meant something powerful and sustaining to Wilfred. It would, he felt, set him free from his family ties, from inherited acquaintances he disliked, from the deadening safeness of his household. But marriage – as an institution which required religious ceremony and the settlement of property – appalled him. Nothing worried him as much as bringing this up with his mother. The more he thought about it the more tense and coarse his feelings became.

'Silly women, damn silly,' he muttered.

'Who are?'

'Oh, I don't know, damn suffragettes. Save Emmeline Pankhurst? Spare her? I'd spare her all right!'

Normally sympathetic to their cause he was now lashing out at the scenes in St Paul's Cathedral the previous Sunday.

'Oh, Wilfred, do understand, for goodness' sake! They think they're taking care of me and in their own way they are. Won't you speak to my father? Or yours first if you like. Won't you?'

Wilfred was furious. His manly feelings were cowed at the prospect of the scenes; he foresaw an explanation in which not only would he not get his own way with his parents but if he was not actually called a young fool and his passion for Eileen designated calf love both would certainly be implied by their every remark. He did not want to face that. Why couldn't Eileen use a bit of tact with hers? In less than four months he was morally Eileen's; he was beginning to love her in a deep, increasingly frantic way; but he had no wish to be bound yet. Life at the Hospital was absorbing, Eileen was absorbing – there was no spare energy to deal with his mother.

'Well, if you think my seeing your father will help to calm them down I will. But you know I'll never get anywhere with my people. We've got to trust each other.'

He felt uneasy. He knew he would be over thirty before he was 'independent' in the sense parents understood.

Especially abhorrent to him was the thought that he should take the quickest way, that of getting into general practice as soon as he could after qualifying, instead of waiting about the Hospital taking all sorts of jobs, nominally paid appointments, until he could get on the staff and later become a specialist, become a Mr Jenkins. Even then it would be years before he could afford to do without some form of allowance from his father. These thoughts troubled him as they approached the station. He became preoccupied and hunched in manner. As the four got into the carriage back to London only the dogs were happy.

* * *

When Wilfred arrived at his home he was deeply tired from overwork. He thought himself up to any crisis until he entered the house. The atmosphere was – well, he simply was young again. His new experience counted for nothing; his knowledge of medical breakthrough and daring discovery evaporated. On this ground battles were fought by never engaging. As Wilfred's eyes moved across the furniture, the firescreen, the portraits, he sensed a defeat in his spirits. The house was as full of quiet rustles as the sideboard was with silver and decanters.

He met his father, spotted tie and yawning, in the doorway to the study.

'My boy, are you well?'

'Yes, thank you, Pater. You and mother?'

'Yes, indeed. Worries, you know, but nothing of note. Getting cold, isn't it? Damn winter settling in.'

'I'll pop up to see Mother if you don't mind. Is she in her room?' Wilfred steadily climbed the steps, trying to compose himself. 'I'm twenty-three. To blazes with all this. I will not scrape. I'm twenty-three. I've seen dead bodies. I've made love to a woman. I'm . . .'

'Good evening, Mater, you look in the pink.'

'Don't be silly, Wilfred,' Mrs Willett said, rubbing her cheek in circular motions. 'You know how tired I am. Everything has been utter confusion lately. I expect your father has told you about our little topple so I won't add anything.'

Wilfred's insides began twisting with pain as if fine wire were being interwoven in his intestines. Could he begin? He determined to be strong. He would just tell her now! Mrs Willett was dipping into one jar and then another. She had not yet turned round from her dressing table although she could see Wilfred in the mirror. Was he to be cowed again by that back, that doctrine of indifference? Without appearing to try, Mrs Willett had discountenanced him. Conversation came spasmodically, circumspect and tactical. Did she know that his heart beat heavily and that his tongue and throat were parched?

'Mater . . . Eileen and I were wondering what you and Father would think of our becoming engaged. I know it's early days yet and we have no real means to talk of, but we are seriously considering it.'

Mrs Willett selected another jar with infinite care and rubbed a little cream into her throat.

'It seems far too early for you and Eileen to embark on anything. It would greatly grieve your father, I know, and I would not feel it right. Why on earth do you want to be engaged? You've only known her a few months.'

'Five months, Mater, and we're desperately fond of each other you know. It seems the right thing to do.'

'It doesn't seem so to your father and mother, Wilfred. Now let me finish before dinner while you go and get dressed.'

Smash the window, pull the curtains down, throw the stool into the road! Wilfred's body tensed and he stared at his mother's back and neck while she casually busied herself. Taut and with difficulty he walked from the room. He firmly shut the door. It was not a slam. Why couldn't he even protest in the well-worn custom? Why didn't he say 'To hell with you and your patronage . . .' Why did he leave lamely?

He sat in his chair back in his room, ashamed and confused. The destruction of his plans was sweeping and he was left feeling stupid. He would leave immediately and moved swiftly to the door and walked downstairs, mumbling to himself.

His father came to the bottom of the staircase, looking up at Wilfred while disdainfully sniffing a glass.

'Ah, there you are. How are things with the sick of the world, eh?' Wilfred could not answer, but his father seemed not to notice.

'Let's have a small one before your mother comes down.'

'No thank you, Pater.'

Mr Willett's eyes registered opposition but withdrew into privacy. Wilfred was going to be difficult and priggish; better let him be than force the issue. He came rarely enough so let him pamper himself with abstinence. Wilfred used to be so sensible but now fluctuated from the extravagant to spoil-sport. It was probably nothing more than the affectation of the student and that Eileen woman. She ministered to Wilfred as if he were some higher being; her manners were unnaturally relaxed. Suddenly there was a whish of silk behind Wilfred and he turned to see his mother.

'Oh, you haven't changed, dear. Well, no matter. I expect you were too tired after your days of endless study. Shall we go in?'

Wilfred managed to last until ten o'clock, his mind alter-
natively enervated and flashing: eggs, life, fowl, deformity,
meat, discharge, claret, cheese, disease. The conversation
moved lightly above him, depicting the swindlers and grand
of London.

'Good night, Mother. Thank you for dinner. Pater.' Moving
behind her chair he kissed his mother on the top of her
head and left abruptly. His father was unusually flurried at
the door.

* * *

As the light was fading early one evening in November,
Wilfred met Eileen after he had spent the whole day at his
studies. They went for a walk down to the river. The curious
light and the taste in the wind brought on a tenderer mood
than they had felt for some days: even the movement of the
craft on the Thames seemed to express their stirrings, the
wharves and the moorings were part of their world. Nothing
was said as their steps slowed. Wilfred knew then that his
medicine would never replace the need for love, the exquisite
anxiety he felt at that moment for Eileen.

Eileen was leaning hard against him, heavy on his shoulder. They knew, without a word, that there was nothing else
needed – virtue, vice, money, the world, what were they?
Eileen wanted Wilfred and had no instinct to think or feel
further. They sat down together, then moved on, no one
knowing or caring who made the decisions. They held hands
between the railings and dropped pieces of gravel into

the blackness below. Suddenly Wilfred broke away, strutting ahead with an imaginary walking stick. Eileen whooped and bounced after him, her slim, tall figure bounding like a rabbit. They felt freed from their moorings, carried firmly by their own skill on the tide.

He stopped and held her close.

'Eileen, we're so lucky. God, we're so lucky.'

'Yes, I know.'

'Today, in one of the wards, I read a letter out to a boy. He asked me to because he couldn't read. He's had his foot crushed and his troop – he's a boy scout – wrote him a collective letter. It was a beautiful letter. I wish I could show it to you but he's tucked it very firmly under his pillow.'

'What's the boy like? How old is he?'

'About twelve. He's so good-looking – blond and very cheeky – and now the little chap'll never be able to play again. You see he talks about football, always football, the whole time. Sister Forsyth calls him "Never-ending". He doesn't know he'll never even kick a ball in the street again.'

'The poor boy. It must be terrible, not being able to do what you want to.'

They walked on in silence.

'Wilfred, don't overwork, darling, will you?'

'Of course not.'

'Sometimes I wonder if you know when the sun is shining.'

'Does it?'

He made her feel warm and resolute.

When they parted, having said very little more in their hour together, they took each other's love into separate beds.

Wilfred was determined to be irrecoverable by his family; his life was beginning to take shape in the way he wanted and not in the mould expected of him. He'd do what he wanted.

Eileen sat with her fingertips on her cheek, then dropped her hand on to her bed. She thought of the night, of the boy scout, of Wilfred's reactions to her concern, of his laughter when she had used her word 'peaky'. Wilfred was a man of extraordinary determination – she could hardly believe the hours he kept. Their toll was clear in his loose arms and restless eyes; the left eye sometimes puckered and pulsed with strain, although it made him very angry to mention it. The main thing was he seemed marvellously happy again. Although Eileen could not understand his hospital work, she did not need to ask: as long as he was absorbed he was fulfilled. She felt she might be able to understand but was frightened that if she tried and couldn't she would be further away.

The vibrations of their love thrilled Wilfred. Sometimes he felt himself weak with desire, throbbing with emptiness of her; and then again he would become morbid and doomed. As a student he needed the emptiness because it kept him unsatisfied, driving him to excessive lengths until he felt cheerfully ill with it all. From this self-denial of the day would come the realisation of evening when he was swallowed up in her. Then he had none of the lounging casual energy which characterised the photographs around his bed: that look of the cultivated, sweet-smelling plant which he had acquired in his youth. Kindled by their growing intimacy they were immune to the winter.

o o o o o o o o

* * *

As he walked out of the Hospital one Thursday in early December, Wilfred seemed confused. He fidgeted, pulling at his gloves, and was occasionally indistinct. He had, not for the first time, hardly eaten all day and was feeling queasy. He decided to go straight to Eileen's although no plans had been made. When he was shown in Eileen stood up suddenly, an alarmed look on her face:

'You look ill, Wilfred. I'll have some food made straight away.'

Mrs Stenhouse went out with Eileen. Wilfred slumped down in a troubled mood, clenching his fists. He lay like that for some minutes with his eyes closed. When Eileen came back he spoke in a strange voice.

'I want to marry you, Eileen.'

She laughed.

'Yes, I know that, darling. But you need your allowance; we've been into all this and I don't mind. It's enough for me as it is. You mustn't upset yourself, oh please don't. I'm all right as I am!'

'Please don't use that phrase.'

'What phrase?'

'"You mustn't upset yourself." You know what it reminds me of.'

Eileen and Wilfred smiled at each other and he took courage again.

'I want to marry you next week. No, I mean it. No one need know. We'll just go along to the Registry Office and walk out, well, married. I've asked about it and it's quite all right. All fixed.'

Wilfred shut his eyes, imitating his father's manner of and-that's-all-there-is-to-it, my old girl. Married. Eileen was really startled but felt her blood beat to the challenge of it. Was it as good as done, just like that? She saw Wilfred run his hand through his brown hair, a tired but controlled gesture. He was desperately in need of sleep, food and comfort – of repose in her. He moved quickly to his feet, agitated.

'Darling, do you mind if I go? I've got to think.'

Over the next few difficult days Eileen tried to retain a calm, understanding influence on Wilfred. She was worried about his cough and rather reckless gestures and yet knew worrying would not help. She saw him whenever she could and only felt frightened when she left him; as long as she was with him she made him secure – her orbit warmed him. Wilfred sold his schoolboy collection of stamps and bought a cheap ring. At eight o'clock on December 16th, they met outside her house and travelled to a Registry Office adjoining a workhouse in a poor street. After a smile of mutual encouragement, they entered the office hand in hand. Quickly and prosaically they were bound man and wife by the law of England, and shook hands with the Registrar. For witnessing the event the office cleaner was given half a crown by Wilfred.

CHAPTER THREE

LONDON 1914

○ ○ ○ ○ ○ ○ ○

The little tables at the bedside reminded him of those at home, except these were not covered with photographs. Photographs! He glanced up at Eileen and thought of Mater at the Royal Tournament – how harmless she seemed to outsiders! He slipped off the bed, lit the gas fire and sank into a chair. Some strange instinct made him want to look through his wallet; he often did this. It was full of important documents and inessentials, things he had no reason to keep but could not throw away. They were part of the wallet.

'Eileen, who was I then? I really can't grasp it.'

'When?'

'Before I met you. Is all the time you spend before you meet the person you love a waste of time, or a preparation or irrelevant?'

'It is an existence. I think most of mine was irrelevant.'

'Why don't you want to know all about me? All the girls I've met, known? What about this girl here? Charming isn't she?'

He motioned to a photograph in his hand.

'Which one?'

'What do you mean, "which one"?'

'I don't think I can ever keep up with all your girls, Wilfred.'

Wilfred enjoyed the way she deflected and deflated his provocation.

'Darling, if Mater knew, if she just knew. I mean Pater would go rigid but the other doesn't bear thinking about. It would be a snorter.'

'Why do you keep such solemn photographs? The people always look so precious in them. I like you now with your tired wise eyes.'

'Loves you too.'

'But why do you keep the photographs?'

'Oh, I don't know.'

He could have given many explanations, even clear and convincing ones, but they wouldn't have been true. He might have said he kept his father's because, in that famous phrase of the Duke of Wellington about the Duke of York, it reminded him of what not to be. That look of Pater's which said 'There you are, Wilfred, I'm afraid I'm right so why argue? I really wouldn't advise an argument, old chap.' He might have said 'Well, Father gives me an allowance – I can't say I love him but he is my father, isn't he?' Wilfred did not want his father erased; he wanted him exposed.

Wilfred and Eileen met in this discreet hotel for a few hours on carefully planned afternoons; it had been difficult to arrange at first but two contacts at the Hospital had mentioned this place in passing to Wilfred, who to ask for and the cost. It was much harder to engineer than the secret marriage and much more fun. In the reflections through the green sunblinds Eileen hushed and soothed him away, leading him from tension through tempest to calm. He often cried afterwards, tears of which he was not ashamed and which it never occurred to him to explain. It was unbelievable, inexplicable. Had he found himself or another or both; or an illusion of any of those which made life worthwhile? In her brown, coppery eyes there was no answer and no need of one.

Wilfred often pestered Eileen about 'the consequences'. She was indeed frightened of having a child but the fear was not as strong as her desire, or rather her obsession. She felt no guilt, no religious scruple. This worried Wilfred who was far more conventional in his Christianity. But her outward calm helped him gain confidence that he was leading their lives into a new, amazing and private world: it felt good from almost the beginning. It felt right: bungling or dexterous, the touching felt right. He was smiling as he thought of it; Eileen laughed across the room at him, tapering into a giggle.

'What are you laughing at?'

'Your mother. She is the pink of elegance, isn't she?'

'And of health, so don't fight with her.'

'I wouldn't, don't worry.'

'Don't. Not with my old mater. She judges by what she sees but don't you make the same mistake. Under the pink she is in battledress.'

They were beside themselves laughing, Wilfred trying to quieten her in case a maid was passing and wondered what on earth was up. 'But what *would* she say if she knew?'

'Well, once we'd brought her round with the salts she'd look up and say: "Wilfred dear, that young lady is not for you, you know. She's a very nice girl, I'm sure, and I know she comes from the very best kind of people, that's obvious I'm glad to say, but you're far too young to know your own mind and not yet settled in the career for which we all have such high hopes. It may seem unpleasant to hear this but the young lady seems to know her own mind far too quickly for your or her own good. You've distressed your father, I'm sure you know that only too well, and I'd be very grateful not to have too much of this subject. It plays havoc with my nerves." Then she'd get up off the chair she'd been fortunate to fall into prior to the salts and call for Rose.'

'Wonderful, wonderful, you've got exactly the right voice. But I don't believe it would be like that in fact.'

'No, nor do I,' said Wilfred. 'It wouldn't be funny. It would be hellish. They'd both go very quiet and controlled and utterly awful. The gaps would widen, that's all, and we'd recover bit by bit over dinner.'

'Has it always been like that?'

'I think so. I've never really thought about anything until this year. I never thought until I met you. When I think of it I went through school and Cambridge in a rather admiring way. Everyone seemed brighter than I was. Nothing seemed surprising about that and I was where I ought to be. It was rather fun but I don't think I was alive.'

'I love listening to you talk. Your words are different from everyone else's, like your hands. Come on, give me your hand.'

One of Eileen's greatest pleasures was reading. As the break with her family was now widening, although still unspoken, she turned increasingly to books. Inspired by Wilfred's self-denying, self-fulfilling hours of study she was determined to read – not only for the imaginative experience, the fun and enjoyment – but because she felt the need for her own special world, her own contribution for Wilfred. She wanted to read to him when they were living together, to tell him about all the novels he would surely read if he weren't so involved with his medicine. He needed this relief.

Wilfred did not, indeed, have time to be a great reader himself but he had a Cambridge eye and ear for the 'likely things'; partly instinctively and partly from a weekly browse through the *Strand* or *The Spectator* he knew the authors worth the money. He laughed at Eileen's taste in Edith Nesbit's stories for children until he read one himself and was delighted by it. Encouraged by this triumph, she told him about Arnold Bennett's *Clayhanger* and the continuation of the story in *Hilda Lessways*. Once, they even decided they would not make love because Eileen's version of the story had captivated him. Nevertheless he was rewarded by a feeling of virtue and unfulfilled desire.

'When do you read, darling?' Wilfred asked.

'But anytime. My days are so empty. What can I do when you're at the Hospital all day? I don't enjoy the talking when you're not with me. It all seems pointless. The conversation is so silly. Everyone either pretends to be good, saying nice things about all our friends – which shows they have no judgment. Or the barriers come down and we have a really nasty squabble. So I take myself off and read. Sometimes I read in my room, sometimes in the study. And always at night in bed.'

'Mmm.'

'While you go to sleep worn out. That must be wonderful too.'

'Sometimes I do. But sometimes I can't settle.'

'Anyway, I've started a new novel. You'd like it I think. *Alice-for-Short* by William de Morgan.'

'Never heard of it or him. Tell me about it. Shortly.'

'You're laughing at me. I won't. I know I don't understand what goes on at the Hospital but you never tell me.'

'Far too tedious. When you understand it loses the fun, the appeal.'

'Don't believe it, Sir Wilfred; why you must be the finest surgeon of all.'

A small cushion narrowly missed a squeaking Eileen.

'Sister, ask the nurse to leave my ward and never return. She is dismissed.'

'But what about the Matron, Sir Wilfred? You know how she dotes on Nurse Stenhouse.'

'Tell the matron to leave this afternoon. Post her to Mrs Thumper.'

Mrs Thumper was their new name for Wilfred's mother.

* * *

The early months of 1914 were full ones, full of walking, talking and work, medicine, ballet and a chill London. There were the high points in their hotel room, and the productions they saw of *Boris Godunov* and *Prince Igor*. Eileen decided to deal with her parents and left Wilfred to his: they met sometimes at Stanhope Gate for brief words, they held hands by the Achilles statue, they could face anything.

March was depressingly wet and on their only night out together in two weeks Eileen was visibly upset: they were in the Queen's Hall, Langham Place, with tickets for a most moving performance of Elgar's Second Symphony, and to Wilfred's distress she was crying during the slow movement. Whispers were answered by a shake of her head: he was told to listen, to stop being silly.

'Nothing, it's nothing, shh please.'

On the way home she told him she might be pregnant. He walked on as many steps as he could without reacting; how many times he had told himself this might happen and if it did, well, it did and there was no point in hysterics. Now it had, might have, happened it seemed less easy to control; it was less a matter of attitude and rationalised position and more a clear case of a very emotional girl. Would his career be ruined, how on earth to deal with both families, what about the allowance? And that pain, God, that pain. Not that.

'But it doesn't matter to me, Wilfred, if you can face it and it doesn't stop you going on with your work.'

She then broke down completely and turned into his chest.

'Don't worry about that for God's sake. I'm sorry, I'm sorry, darling. When will you know, for sure I mean?'

'I don't know. A few days or a week or whatever – I'm not sure.'

'You really mustn't worry too much. Yes, I know that's damned easy to say, but I don't care what anyone says and I'll look after you.'

It was a short-lived fear. Two days later a strained voice told Wilfred on the telephone that 'all is well' and things went on as before.

On June 5th, Eileen's house was agog at the 'goings-on' at Court. Two years previously Eileen and Victoria had been 'presented', an occasion they would never forget, despite waiting for an hour and a half, and spending only twenty seconds in the Royal presence. But something really had happened this time. The *Daily Mail* and *The Times* carried headlines: Lady Blomfield's daughters protested to the King about 'forcible feeding' of the suffragettes in prison. The chanting 'Save Emmeline Pankhurst' in St Paul's the previous autumn had infuriated Mrs Thumper; the offensive behaviour to the King (at His Majesty's Theatre of all places) in May was unforgivable in the Stenhouse rooms; but this incident interested even Eileen who had remained very detached throughout the various pressures and hysteria of the whole campaign.

'And then Lady Blomfield fainted?' she was saying as Wilfred entered their drawing room.

'Oh, good evening, Wilfred,' Mrs Stenhouse called from the chaise-longue. She had been sufficiently moved by the Court scandal to lay down her racing paper. It was for her the first serious incident in 1914. 1913 had contained two incidents: Emily Davison's bringing down of the King's 'Anmer' at Tattenham Corner on which Mrs Stenhouse had £5. That the horse was near the back had never been the point; horses had won from that position before. And a few days later a potty Old Harrovian had fallen in front of the favourite for the Gold Cup; Mrs Stenhouse had not backed the favourite but she might have done. And now this outrage.

'But why wasn't Lady Blomfield with them?'

'She didn't know her daughters were there, poor thing. And what a disgrace they were. She had decided, obviously quite rightly, to leave them at home because she knew they were up to something. They were "keen on Emmeline" as they disgustingly put it.'

'Well, how did they get in?' Victoria asked. 'They were very strict on our tickets.'

'And so they should have been this time. What is the country coming to? It appears they talked their way in and when one of them was actually on the point of being presented she said "Stop forcible feeding." Quite disgraceful!'

'It says here, Mama, that Sir Douglas Dawson led them away. And the "other" Lady Blomfield wishes to reassure her friends that she is only distantly related to the perpetrators of this insult to the King.'

Wilfred agreed it was a tasteless, silly thing to do.

'Silly, Wilfred? Silly? I am not against some of the suffragettes, demented though they are. But this is more than silly. It's outrageous.'

Wilfred thought it was more than silly but stuck to his word. Was it as outrageous as being married to your daughter, madam, when you don't even know it? Was it as outrageous as winking at the porter in the Osborne Hotel and going into Room 11 from 2 to 4.30 and then home to the Stenhouses for a demure tea? Was it? His hands moistened – they must find out some day, probably before too long. He looked across at Eileen who looked as if she were in the other room.

* * *

Eileen had found sufficient reserves to visit the Willetts on wet Sundays, when Wilfred often suggested billiards as a way of avoiding tense discussions. His over-technical teaching made very little impression on Eileen's performance and only her sweetness and the well-known curve of her lithe body as she leant across the table to play yet another gruesome shot helped to keep him from being disagreeable. Mrs Thumper took these opportunities to make rather a point of asking other girls in for tea, although it was perfectly obvious that Wilfred and Eileen's relationship had long passed the stage where counter-attractions would matter one jot; of course she knew this as well as anyone but it was a matter of pride that she would never yield an inch till they had walked to the altar. And that, she was quite right, they had not yet done. Eileen was amused that Mrs Thumper should treat her as a seductive adventurer who had waylaid her Wilfred; perhaps if she had been a pretty barmaid or an actress Mrs Thumper would have been more confident in buying her off. Such a move was not beyond her if the cause was saving her favourite boy. The lovers breathed deeply on these occasions, watching the well-worn game unfold. It was at least material for later jokes, unfunny as it was.

On better days Eileen greatly enjoyed watching Wilfred fish. Here his strength, agility and swift gestures engrossed her. She sat by the side of a lovely little river dangling her toes, looking at a stretch of tiny rapids on the bend where the wind stroked the spear leaves of the tall willows. He caught small trout with a fly or fished for roach with the same ambition and single-mindedness of the hospital. To see him like that was as satisfying as making love to him. The setting was perfect; there was no tedious ground-baiting, no waiting hour after hour and yet just enough waiting to lend anticipation and thrill to the catch. The bank was in its natural state. No places had been worn smooth by feet of frequent swimmers.

By teatime Wilfred would often have a good basket of thick olive-coloured backs, displaying them to her.

'Oh Wilfred. How splendid and clever of you!'

They tramped happily back a mile and a half to the main road, passing through cornfields in which poppies were beginning to grow. Wilfred's deep interest in nature and considerable knowledge of birds and flowers made the walks in the country special; rabbits bobbed and nosed in the grass – these people were quite rare. Unashamedly, and with an increasing abandon, Wilfred and Eileen were in love.

* * *

It would not be quite true to say that the war rumours had not filtered into Wilfred's mind but he had certainly not been infected by the mounting hysteria of late July. One night, however, he went with some other students to hear Asquith speak at the Albert Hall and suddenly grasped the menacing European situation. The Balkan wars and the Naval Estimates had been small matters in comparison; even Ireland. The papers he read at breakfast talked of closing the ranks, the brink of this or that, and waning hopes; the streets were full at unusual hours of the day, and editions of the papers increased in regularity. Incredibly, he became one of the jostling mob who shared the mounting horror and indignation over the Archduke Franz Ferdinand and that 'dreadful business' at Sarajevo. Eileen pressed him to explain it all to her: he couldn't and wouldn't, wasn't it perfectly clear? Within days he had changed; he was reacting in just the way he scorned in others – he was reacting as someone of his background could be expected to. He realised what he 'must do' but overlaid with fear of telling Eileen and fear of breaking off his studies at the Hospital he let the days slip by. But if the 'officers were going' and the fleet were putting to sea, why wasn't he doing his job too? He must. However dislocated his life, he must!

The telephone was answered and eventually Eileen came. Her voice was soft and questioning for the first few moments; as his drift became clear she moved on to a higher pitch of determination. When he put forward his plan she was exasperated most of all by his tone of 'more than that I can't say', the very conceited and patronising tone of his father, the tone Wilfred mocked so often.

'You sound just like your father.'

'That's not the point. Do be reasonable.'

'I'm coming to see you. You can't just throw everything up like this. I'm coming to see you. It's mad.'

'Oh do be sensible, Eileen. You know I love you. I don't want you to come, it would be silly.'

'I'm coming,' she said, and put down the telephone. She had never been so upset in her life. Her face was wretched with indignation and strain – this immediately clashed with Wilfred's somewhat buoyant and jubilant assertiveness and in five minutes they were arguing. To her he seemed entirely different, transformed, as if his personality had been put into a straitjacket. To him, she was unaware of the seriousness of the situation and the special need for people who were trained in the OTC to give a lead; she irritated him by mentioning his career and examinations.

'There'll be plenty of time for those. It really is my duty. You must try to see that. I'm amazed you can't.'

After some minutes of pomposity and petulance Wilfred calmed into a measure of reason. Eileen, too, moved towards an accepting tone; they softened in each other's fears. But as they walked out together from his home she stirred even deeper pride.

'Darling, if this is the case isn't it time we told our people we're married?'

There had been no approach to this, and Wilfred exploded as if he had been hit.

'God, no! That's the last thing. This business can't last long, you know that as well as I do. You know I want you. Why ruin it all by telling them anything they needn't know?'

The issue was painfully personal to Eileen. She did not want to have a wounded husband, or be a widow; she did not want to be in a powerless position. If 'anything happened' to Wilfred she wanted to be the one who helped. Words previously unused by them entered their argument – sacrifice, idealism, death, compromise, selfishness – the words that stick, infect and fester. Wilfred behaved boorishly; he took it all in very bad grace.

Finally he conceded. While away for two days at Cambridge, where he made arrangements to join his regiment in late August, he wrote to both sets of parents briefly explaining what had happened the previous December and that as he might be about to leave the Hospital for the Army he felt they 'should know'. When he returned all insisted on the soonest possible day for the marriage in church; his father had replied by letter, left on Wilfred's bedside table.

I am very glad you have had the courage to tell me, rather late though it now is. We have forgiven you but there are certain things that must be done. First and foremost you and Eileen must be properly married in church, and until that is the case you will not of course stay with her in this house. That Eileen should have married you in a registry office and have had no church service distressed both your mother and me very much. That must, as I have said, be remedied. I shall not at present discontinue your allowance although when you begin to receive your Army pay I may have to reconsider this in the light of the situation as it develops.

Although you may not have anything much to leave it may also be advisable to make a will. I look forward to seeing you on your return.

Your loving pater

Indiscriminately despising himself Wilfred went on the day decided straight to the church in Queen's Gate. As the morning service was not yet over he knelt down to pray for Eileen, for forgiveness, for safety in battle, for Eileen, for Eileen. He looked to the left through his fingers and saw her, tall, composed and beautiful, entering the side door with her father. He sat up and waited for his parents. Eventually his father slipped into the pew:

'Is Mater coming?'

'My dear boy, she's far too upset, do try to understand. Have you got a ring?'

'I think Eileen's father has.'

'Have you got a best man?'

'No.'

'Then I shall be glad to do so.'

And so before that small, unhappy group they were married. The old priest, incoherent from a recent stroke, mumbled the words into his beard and Wilfred was regularly prompted by his father. The responses went into the dark roofing, all sunlight obscured by the tall, close-up buildings which surrounded the church. On their right the verger's black gown seemed minatory. Only Eileen in a white cotton dress for summer and white straw hat relieved the scene; she lifted her olive, oval face to him and firmly pressed his hand. He could not respond.

There was no reception and they spent 'their night' depressed and alone – each in the usual bedroom. Next day *The Times* court page carried the respectable facts.

* * *

The long August days between leaving the Hospital and joining the London Rifle Brigade were difficult ones for Wilfred. He found himself awake very early in the morning, his mind racing and confused, trying to discipline his thoughts into a clear plan of action. Every day he used much of his emotional energy in explaining to Eileen that he was taking the right course. They met at various times for long walks, wherever their fancy took them, through streets even more crowded than usual – excited groups, lively twos and threes gathering to discuss the day's developments, peering at various editions of each paper.

Wilfred took Eileen through the Park. Quick conversations alternated with long periods of silence. To Wilfred the war was to be a short but necessary break in his studies; necessary because he was young, fit, trained and needed. (He had been through this so many times in his mind and too often, for his patience, with Eileen.) To Eileen it simply meant Wilfred was going away, possibly not to return. She wanted to discuss this possibility but he did not.

Although on the surface the last year with her family had been as normal, civilised and restrained, as usual, she felt herself now being increasingly tense and touchy. Eileen had, of course, both before and after the marriage, been under no illusions that Wilfred was approved of. Indeed she had some sympathy with their disapproval because she knew they were not able to understand and she had made no effort to explain (in terms that they would understand) her passion and obsession. What her mother and her elder sisters had felt for their men before marriage and what they now felt she could only guess at; she very much doubted their intimate lives were as satisfactory as hers. Was the war going to shatter this satisfaction and other delights?

Her fear of pregnancy before the 'official' marriage in church had not stopped her wanting Wilfred whenever the opportunity arose. Eileen had always been superstitious about all this. In many cases it was of the normal kind – dates and phrases – but she was now disturbed by green in any form. Superstition may well give some poetry to life; Eileen, however, knew it was going too far. The more she tried to avoid green the more she came into contact; the faster she ran away the quicker she ran into it. Whenever Wilfred wore green she was sure something dreadful would happen; a green stitch on the eiderdown made her mood change. And the uniform!

They were walking in the Park, not (as Wilfred remarked) perhaps the best place to discuss her dominant superstition.

'Wilfred, you will check through all your clothing before you go to Crowborough, won't you?'

'Of course, darling, but don't worry so much. You really do go too far. I'll write to you every day. Perhaps I'll kill green for you in France.'

Wilfred immediately regretted this feeble remark, the last thing to placate her.

'But you're not definitely going to France, are you?'

'I don't know. But I should think it's likely. I shouldn't think they could keep the LRB out of it for long.'

'You don't want to go, do you?'

'Well, apart from you and the Hospital, yes – I mean if no one went what would happen?'

'But thousands do want to go. Look at them. Every day. They seem to be clamouring for a chance to go. No one would miss you.'

He turned to Eileen. He took her hand.

'The trouble is I don't think I could stay. If I felt I was avoiding it, I couldn't enjoy anything. We argued about this last Thursday in the Hospital. Quite a few of them thought I was wrong. I don't want to be pig-headed but I think it's the right thing.'

'Can I come to see you at Crowborough? You can't just go away like this.'

'I hope you can. I don't know the arrangements. This is my first war, you see.'

'Don't joke. Not at the moment, please.'

'We'll be under canvas in Crowborough but I'll try to find a room for you somewhere.'

They stopped and sat down. People walked along the paths: men striding through to an appointment, old men alone, nurses with children, lovers blind to the world and locked in confessional attitudes. It was nearing lunchtime on a beautiful clear day; holding hands very tightly they looked at all the passers-by. Eileen touched his lean, firm body; she sensed his quick, energetic movements; she stroked his clear

skin, so pale from indoors. Wilfred took his hand away to pre-
pare a pipe. She loved watching this because Wilfred was
preoccupied in a precise way. The tobacco was selected, every
piece as if he was prejudiced against all others; with his long
expert fingers rolling and stroking as he packed it in. Finally
he lit the pipe and lay back, cradling his head with his left
hand.

They both felt happy in a fragile, aching way: the warmth
suffused them with well-being. The moments were memorised
as they were experienced; as Eileen lay back she thought this
meeting may have to be a 'calming down' drug in the weeks
of separation ahead. It was a disturbing realisation. Would she
wake up one morning to find it all over?

As she put her knife into the butter at breakfast, could
she tell her mother what she felt about 'her husband'? Could
she tell her sisters? If Wilfred was killed would he then be
conjured into a hero, made acceptable by death? Eileen pulled
herself up on to her elbows and looked down at Wilfred. His
eyes remained neutral, unfocused on the bluish distance. She
wanted to be parted in loss and not linked for ever by loss.

Wilfred tapped his pipe, watching the small embers burn
the grass, destroying a little fear, the warm smell coming to his
nostrils. Eileen was already standing, stretching a hand down
to bring him to his feet.

'Let's go or we'll both be late for lunch.'

'When shall we meet this afternoon? Shall we go to an
exhibition?'

'I'd love to. You decide.'

They walked back at a leisurely pace, possessed by each

other, each already coming to terms with the new situation. The most unexpected and unwanted things were always a challenge to Eileen. Like Wilfred she went to meet them before they knocked her off balance.

* * *

They found it hard to believe, as they looked at the Summer Exhibition at the Royal Academy, that war had been declared. It had been a remarkable summer for them. Wilfred had been working through vital stages of his Hospital training; they had converged with thousands of people on Hyde Park for the National Union of Suffrage demonstration; they had met and loved; they had been through their second wedding ceremony, traditional and 'fitting', and as unsatisfactory as the first. Their freedom had not been complete, nor had their occasional compliance with conformity been pleasing either to their families or themselves.

As they walked around the gallery, a married couple doubly proved, they had never had a full day under the same roof; they had never openly shared the same bed and breakfast table. They had never said 'Good night' to the remainder of either family and gone upstairs together. And now after those months of wearing secrecy they were no nearer that lasting security which Eileen thought Wilfred needed if he was to be happy and successful in his work.

'Wilfred, they weren't very helpful at lunch. I tried twice to explain about you going away and how I wanted to visit you. No one thought it a good idea.'

'Look, we're married. I know we don't live together yet but as soon as I've qualified all this will be over. Don't worry about them.'

'I've got to see you again soon. Let's find out train times so I can leave on the spot if I have to. Which station is it for Crowborough?'

Wilfred was slightly irritated by Eileen's persistence because it reflected on his wavering confidence and yet elated that she should want him so much. He wanted to hug her, crush her in his arms, there in front of the pictures. Quietly he took her by the elbow and walked out into the street. The sun was very hot now. They felt the pavements through their shoes, and the air heavy with city smells.

They stepped out of the taxicab about one hundred yards from the Osborne Hotel and walked towards it. Neither spoke. Twenty yards from the hotel Wilfred turned left and strode on. He glanced at Eileen: she was a little dejected but not as much as he hoped. He squeezed her hand and smiled openly.

'Let's go to my parents for tea.'

'Oh, Wilfred, please. I can't take that today. Please don't ask me to.'

'Oh, come on. You and Mrs Thumper – we three for tea.'

Eileen was pale with anger. She stopped him within thirty yards of his front door.

'Wilfred, any other time. But don't ruin a lovely day. I did enjoy the Gallery, darling, and the walk and everything.'

'Don't be silly. We've got to face up to her. I'll see you through.'

Wilfred led up the steps and opened the door. Eileen followed, a mixture of pain and pride on her face. 'Come on in, darling,' he shouted over his shoulder, unnaturally loud and confident. He had never been like this before and Eileen was upset – his masterful, bullying tone did not suit him – he had become almost ugly.

'Now I wonder where Mater is. Mater! Hang on while I find Rose. Rose! Where is everyone?' Wilfred moved in and out of the rooms, only stopping to glance.

'Wilfred, please let's go. Now, while there's time. I don't think I'm up to it. I'm feeling rather sick.'

Eileen turned back towards the front door. A sudden whoop of laughter held her on her turn.

'They've all gone. They've gone, gone, gone.' Wilfred was almost hysterical, leaping up the stairs in twos. He sat on the landing and looked down at Eileen.

'Are you serious? Where are they? Where's Rose, the servants? Gone where?'

'It's Rose's day off, the other two have a holiday, and . . . And Pater and Mrs Thumper have have . . . have . . .'

He played with Eileen's feelings, shouting at her through the banisters, torturing her, 'have . . . have . . . gone away for a week to their August hotel in Eastbourne.' He fell on to his back laughing.

Eileen moved towards the foot of the stairs. As she climbed up, she spoke a word on each step, moving faster and faster towards Wilfred.

'It's – just – too – good – to – be – true – I – love – you – Wilfred – even – when – you – play – tricks.' Wilfred came down to her.

Seventeen steps and into his arms.

* * *

The next morning at a late breakfast Wilfred talked to Rose about joining the LRB and his attitude to the few days left. He had also long wanted to explain to this old friend his feelings about his 'marriage' but he had not found the appropriate moment: either his parents were in the room, or he felt it too obvious to search out Rose on the 'off-chance'. As she brought in his tea he said, as casually as he could, 'Well, it won't be long now, I'm afraid, so I hope the toast is good.' Rose continued bustling about as she replied,

'I'll miss you, I will. But perhaps it won't be too long. They say it'll be a short one and they'll know, I'm sure.'

Wilfred wasn't so sure, but decided against that speculation.

'If my wife calls round when I'm away you will be nice to her, won't you, Rose? She's had an awful time – perhaps you blame me, I don't know – but I hope she won't feel unwanted. I'm afraid my mother doesn't take to her and Father may not be in.'

'Miss Eileen need fear nothing from me, sir. I've always said she was a very delightful young lady.'

'Do you think we were wrong to marry like that, in secret? Oh, come on, you must have heard. I expect you know all about it. And how that's why we didn't have a reception.'

Wilfred did want to 'tell' Rose all, to justify his actions in a fairly frank and amusing manner. He felt his words begin to flow in a skilful way, and he rather enjoyed listening to himself in this vein. It was fairly accurate history and yet made more lively and impressive by shaping anecdotes and clinching self-justifications. At school he was liked for his wit and stories at his own expense. He talked non-stop for about ten minutes while Rose stood, her hands clenched on the back of the chair, following every word. She interrupted twice with gestures towards his tea and food, which he gulped before hurrying on.

'So you can see how miserable it is for Eileen, Rose. We've been married nearly a year and no one seems to approve. Even now we're still apart and I'm off to the War.'

'Well, it's not good enough. Now if you would like to bring Miss Eileen round today or tomorrow for something to eat, I'd really like to look after you two, I would. In the afternoon I've got to go over to see my sister about a few things she needs doing. You will write to me when you're away, won't you? That card you sent from Cambridge once telling me you'd been up in an aeroplane!'

Wilfred looked at her with unashamed affection. All his life he had learnt to control his feelings, especially with those not quite in his line. As he pushed in his chair and moved next to Rose she collected up the plates and walked determinedly off to the kitchen.

They had arranged to meet at Harrods. The trappings of the wedding had irritated him as much as his behaviour made him squirm with shame – he could be walking along the road or shaving when the memory of it, so keen, came back. He would buy her something which she happened to see and never dreamed he could afford. Although Eileen was rich and could have dressed in striking and fashionable clothes, her taste was simple and elegant. She had no desire to emulate the girls in the square who stepped out in high style. He had noticed, however, that she pointed out unusual rings and necklaces, greys, lilacs, pinks and browns – not particularly expensive, perhaps, but ones which were quietly interesting and subtle if looked at for a while. These rings and necklaces always blended skilfully with her eyes, hair and skin.

As Eileen saw him approaching she ran up to him, so excited he nearly thought he'd been invited to stay with the Stenhouses. He did the thing he knew she most loved: he did not react and looked coolly around himself. 'Well,' he said. 'Where do we start?'

This put him in command and yet apparently on her orders. She squeezed his arm and skipped away, with Wilfred standing there, grinning reluctantly.

'You old fraud, you,' she laughed. 'How is the Willett home without the Willetts?'

'Beautifully full of you and me. My room will never be the same. And don't forget beautiful, wonderful Rose.'

'Why? What has she done?'

'I'll tell you later. But first of all would the belle of Ashburn Place show a young man of small means the varied pleasures of this delectable establishment?'

She curtsied slightly, which turned a few stiff heads that passed, and did as she was bid. Room after department, floor by floor, they pulled each other, stopping to gaze, peering at each other from opposite sides. Eileen popped her head between two hatstands; Wilfred tried two walking sticks and threatened her with a 'rare old beating, young madam'. Eileen threw up her eyebrows and moved on.

The jewellery counter was now in sight. Wilfred controlled his face into studied indifference, not exactly whistling, and asked Eileen what else there was to see.

'But just a quick look at the jewellery, could we?'

'Of course. Sorry, I wasn't thinking.'

Wilfred took out his pocketbook and jotted down one or two lines of nonsense, taking furtive glances at Eileen. She paused a few times and once looked back at him. He happened to change his feet and lounged even more against the wall. She paused again and leant over, peered, stood upright, reassessed, moved on a few yards, turned back. Wilfred sauntered nearer, saw what Eileen was looking at and hurried the final three paces.

'And what can I do for madam?'

'Ah, kind sir, madam is keen on that one.'

'But madam will prove a wrecker to men and no less, bringing disgrace upon her family, if she wears that. But if that's what madam wants.'

Eileen was delighted with Wilfred's mood. He had lost his old preoccupation and tension; they were still warm from the previous day's love, closely bound by Wilfred's bedroom. As they walked out of the jewellery department, Wilfred said, 'Wait here a moment, darling. I won't be long.'

He doubled back and went straight to the counter. 'Excuse me, my wife would like that pendant. I think I'll take it.'

'Yes, sir. This is five pounds, seventeen shillings and sixpence, sir.'

'Thank you. What is it made of?'

'Diamonds and amethysts, sir.'

Wilfred paid and caught up with Eileen.

'What was all that about?'

'I wanted to have another look at something.'

'Where shall we go now? I've told them I'm out with you for the day.'

'Rose's getting the lunch for us at home. She said she wanted us both to "have a quiet little time together". Forcible feeding with the Willetts!'

'Oh, how perfect.'

'And then Rose has to visit her sister to see to a few things.'

Eileen suddenly looked frightened.

'Wilfred, it's going so well I'm worried. It's so lovely with you. It will last, won't it? You'll be careful, really, terribly careful, won't you?'

'Of course, I don't want to lose you.'

Wilfred distracted Eileen's attention to a tin on another counter.

'Bond's Plugite – white self vulcanising outer cover stopping that won't come out. Has no disgusting smell . . . "For Mrs T!" ' They laughed at that and at an old brass Italian bedstand ('only £10 15s.!'). On his way out Wilfred's eye caught:

'Officer's Regulation Yeltra Waterproof £3 3s.' But he had spent all he had on the pendant.

* * *

London was in a state of manic excitement. The Stock Exchange was closed, the Bank Rate was up, everyone was worried. Wilfred was astonished to read the National Penny Bank was 'closed until further notice'. On his way to see Eileen one day, just before joining his regiment, he met an old woman crying, in Gloucester Road.

'Will it ever open again, sir, will it?'

Wilfred, tender and embarrassed, comforted her and said all would be well. As he walked away he realised why he had been asked: for the first time he was wearing uniform. Later that day there were vast crowds in Whitehall and Trafalgar Square. Everywhere he went people shook hands with him until he ached: he received hundreds of polite and touching remarks. As he moved up some steps he saw a mob of over thirty hounding someone.

'What's going on there?' he asked.

They turned and gabbled out accusations about a little man, cowering fifteen yards away.

'Leave him alone.'

They muttered something about Germans and the man ran off.

'Well, he's gone now. Will someone give me a light for my pipe?' Wilfred was given one and like lambs they moved on.

'Funny what a uniform will do,' said a policeman behind Wilfred. Wilfred smiled and nodded goodbye. He crossed the square and walked on, while behind him he could hear what seemed a thousand men singing.

'Are we downhearted? No! No! No!' – to the tune of 'Sun of My Soul' . . . He felt strangely strong and weak.

* * *

The Regiment was camped on some high hills. They were expected to be there for at least the first three weeks of September, training in all aspects of infantry warfare – but most of all getting fit. Wilfred took the first opportunity to write to Eileen, asking her to come, no matter how; they would find somewhere to lodge her. The adjutant said he knew a local woodman who had told him he had a spare room if any officer needed it.

In the evening Wilfred set out for the woodman's, deeply moved by the beauty of the surrounding country – noticing everything, the birds and flowers with an extra sensitivity and joy. The cottage reminded him strongly of Marty South's; and the woodman was indeed as like a Hardy character as could be imagined – strong, fine-boned, tanned, undemonstrative, of the soil and the place. It seemed so appropriate for their love, a natural room for quiet passion. Wilfred pressed the man to put a price on the offer and was firmly told he could leave what he felt like when the room was no longer needed. It was an idyll.

Wilfred drove himself to exhaustion each day, determined to be the most efficient officer in the regiment. Indeed, he tended to be a martinet, more strenuous than was even good for morale, carrying the packs of those who were tired and gaining in reward a subtle mixture of gratitude and distaste.

No one liked being helped in public in that period of frenzied patriotism. Wilfred often gave away his food and drink because he could do without; he was also concerned to show that officers could be above petty authority and scornful methods. He would not write notes about the missing latrine bucket – he would find it himself. If anyone had told him this was thought a kind of ostentation as irritating as more punitive measures he would have been shocked. A deep vein of idealism ran through him.

The regiment was beginning to hear a few stories of events across the Channel. Although there were no broadcasts or official press communiqués there were already daily casualty lists. More importantly, there was growing a dim understanding that this was not a play where only fit young men and appropriate behaviour would score – although as yet it was an understanding seen in the eyes and not heard. It was apparently healthy, jolly and satisfying; underneath they knew it would not be playing soldiers.

Each day was demanding; infantry training, sessions studying Field Service Regulations, pack marches. Suddenly a simple note arrived for Wilfred: 'Will be with you at 6 p.m. Eileen.'

Walking with Eileen on the edge of the wood which looked down on the camp, Wilfred was happy but could not strike the right chord. The first glimpse of him in uniform in London had made her almost droop with despair and unspoken foreboding and these feelings now returned. As his glorious, forced holiday atmosphere began to wane she turned to him:

'How long will you be here, Wilfred?'

'Three weeks. We leave for France in four.'

'When did you hear?'

'This morning. Everyone's very proud. We're the first Territorial Regiment to be chosen.'

A squirrel scampered over the road. Wilfred stood still, watching the brown, leaping, hesitating flash jump from bough to bough until it was lost in the canopy of the wood. Wilfred picked up one of the cones, looking closely at the shredding the squirrel had done. He had found his interest in nature at St Paul's and as a sixteen-year-old he had lectured to the Field Society on angling and later on 'Birds in Sussex'. He wanted not only to enjoy the squirrels' colour and variety; he wanted to know their secrets. He turned and handed the cone to Eileen. 'From one squirrel to another,' he said smiling. Eileen tried to smile back but was not interested. Her face was tolerant, like a grown-up viewing a child's enthusiasm for something so well known.

Two weeks later Wilfred's parents came down to have lunch with him, arranging to meet at the best local hotel. Wilfred was so involved with his military life and Eileen that, despite past evidence, he felt this meeting would heal everything. If he was going into the firing line against fearful odds surely all bitterness would disappear, new ties be established between the four of them? He strode along with Eileen and turned briskly into the hotel doors. They were not in sight. A porter came up and said Mr and Mrs Willett would be waiting in the dining room. As Wilfred led Eileen across the rooms, unsure whether to hold her arm or not (he didn't), he forced his hand out towards his father although his knees were 'going'.

'Eileen dear, so you've come to say goodbye too?'

'Not exactly, Mrs Willett, I've been staying for the last few weeks near Wilfred's camp.'

There was no need for an augury: Mr Willett was puzzled, brooding over the menu, while Mrs Thumper looked as if someone had taken her seat at the theatre.

'Really? Is that suitable? It must be very uncomfortable.'

'Oh no. The people are very kind. Their son has gone to France too.'

'Well, dear, all I can say is it must be nice to be so young, and so easily pleased. Now what will you eat, Wilfred? Oh I'm sorry, you haven't finished with the menu.' Mrs Willett waited with a threatening patience.

Wilfred looked at Eileen. She looked at him and placed her clenched fist on the table – the thumping sign. Well, once again Wilfred had miscalculated in expecting any development in understanding but at least they could still see the funny side. He hoped. He suddenly felt that strange enervation again, as if things were slipping out of his control, and immediately fell into rather inane remarks about relieving the troops, lines of communication, regiments 'trained like ours' and so on. He sensed the information was not only decidedly fatuous but also not at all what they came down to hear. Only politeness listened. He could hear his old English master saying 'Oh, Willett, how can you be so *jejune*?'

Throughout lunch Eileen was outcast, deliberately dispossessed of her lover and husband by detailed reference to members of the Willett family, members so remote that Wilfred had hardly heard of them for years. All of a sudden, it seemed, they were sending Wilfred their love and respect as he took on the enemy. Through this patter the ordering of the meal was punctilious and the wine judicious. It seemed to Wilfred the event would have no ending unless his parents were to take their afternoon nap after an exhausting journey down. Without a nap the afternoon would be agony; and he wanted Eileen. His frequent looks to reassure and question Eileen's moods were unnecessary – she was self-possessed and uncomplaining. She half-smiled, barely a reaction; unprotected she may be but she knew a battle was on. Her behaviour turned what might have been ghastly into the merely tiresome. Wilfred was immensely grateful because he could not bear a row at this stage. Why had so many meals in his life been painful? Was it that they were the only times when he and his parents talked?

'You will write, dear, won't you? We shall be anxious for you.'

'Of course, Mother, and you'll see lots of Eileen now won't you, as often as . . . (damn, damn, damn) . . . and you'll both be getting news of me.'

'If Eileen calls in the afternoons, dear, and I'm in I'll be only too glad to see her.'

Eileen put her hand to her pendant and ran her slim fingers along it. She transmitted to Wilfred 'Don't worry. Let her say what she likes. I love you. Telegraph the dreadful news to your father because he's going to sleep.'

Long before the porter told the Willetts their car was waiting Wilfred had considered abject capitulation along the 'I'm dreadfully to blame and so's Eileen, aren't you, darling, and please forgive me before I go off to die' lines, but Eileen remained steady. Wilfred instead pulled himself up for one last massive deception, and did it very thoroughly.

'How lovely of you to come down today. It's really helped having you here at this rather, well you know, difficult time.'

Wilfred even found himself stammering with a kind of surplus emotion, as if he were taking leave of a master he'd never liked and found himself overcome with a muddled mixture of shame and regret.

'We'll be thinking of you, dear.'

'Rather! And good luck, my boy. God bless!'

They'd gone. Turning from the door Wilfred felt so released he considered indulging a little self-pitying drama. He stood holding the back of Eileen's chair and said in a somewhat thunderous voice, 'Let's go for a walk,' and setting his jaw looked down at Eileen. She was openly laughing at his histrionics.

'Oh, darling, don't be silly. You look as if you're in a pulpit. You're much more pleased that they're gone than angry with what happened. And don't be angry with yourself because you were marvellous. It was gruesome though, wasn't it?'

'You were the marvellous one. You positively swam.'

Wilfred dropped the idea of a temper, his touchiness evaporated in her warmth. Nevertheless they did go for a walk, a gloriously happy one with no striding masculinity. It was the best kind of walk, aimless but involving, apparently endless. Wilfred was pointing out this or that, explaining the hedgerows, pulling off twigs and threatening Eileen with them. 'It has been decided to chastise you, woman.' They roamed over the hills for two hours, strong, careless and defiant again against the world. Even debris, pieces of wood and bone became fascinating for a moment.

The regiment was to entrain for Southampton the next morning and everyone had been ordered to spend the Sunday night in camp. Set free from his parents Wilfred found courage to ask the Colonel in rather erratic phrases whether there was any chance of an exception being made. He made this request while they were walking to the mess. As the Colonel stopped in the doorway Wilfred hurriedly supported his case with the fact that he had done two Saturday nights' extra duty.

'Haven't you read the orders, Willett?'

'Yes, sir.'

'Aren't you a good enough officer to do your duty without having me to tell you?'

They went in, the Colonel breathing rather petulantly. Suddenly he turned to Wilfred.

'Mind you're on parade at seven tomorrow. I shall see you then. Good night!'

Wilfred was quite exhilarated. He had caught an old glance, learnt at school, in which authority said 'And what you do between now and then is your own affair, as long as I don't hear of it.' He walked slowly away, controlling his anticipation, telling himself not to hurry ahead into an imaginary bed – not to build it up too much. Too many failures and let-downs came that way; this time it was going to be mature, perfect.

Half carrying Eileen, Wilfred went upstairs. The room was dark, small and warm even at that late hour. By the candlelight they eased on to the bed, and under the blanket and into each other. Quiet and tender they did not want to destroy with passion, afraid of too much. They did not worry about a child; they cared only for each other and that night. They cried afterwards, alone and together; full of sorrow they lay talking quietly till dawn. Eileen ran her fingers over him gently, movements of confidence, establishing his presence, imprinting her touch and mind on to his firm body. At six o'clock they went for a walk in the wood, skirting around any view that led them to see their destination. At a quarter to seven they looked down through the mists on the bustling, flapping camp. It had seemed so far away in the dark.

CHAPTER FOUR

PLOEGSTEERT

○ ○ ○ ○ ○ ○ ○

October 3rd, 1914

Darling Eileen,

We arrived in France yesterday. I must say the disembarking was a tedious business and the progress through the town to the rest camp was the worst march I've ever experienced. Not at all what we expected in Crowborough! We did frequent checking but allowed no halts and this taught us the true weight of our packs. How much I wanted to write to you and then read one of my books! When we arrived at the camp there was another inspection which completed the exhaustion.

On landing it was learnt that we officers were no longer to wear 'Sam Browne' belts or to carry swords. So there was a frantic rush at the last moment to find web equipment before we caught the train. We left our belts and hats at the base camp.

I am missing you most dreadfully. The days – it is only two – seem longer than ever but I must not seem 'down' to the others. If you will write as often as you can it will make everything worthwhile. Please address your letters to General Headquarters where we are due to arrive tomorrow.

My hopes of having a comfortable journey were dampened by this sign on the train 'Hommes 40 Chevaux (en long) 8'. My suspicions were aroused and we indeed have many hours to spend in this train.

Oct. 5th

Many hours! It was over twenty and when we arrived here, tired but hopeful, no arrangements had been made. The Battalion was not even expected. Do not tell the parents as they would not believe it and be upset. After arriving, we had to stay in the train for three hours before moving into old artillery barracks. They are so dirty and dismal but there is rumour we're going into a convent tomorrow! If only my favourite were there.

I love you,
Wilfred

10th Oct. 1914

Darling Eileen,

We are in Belgium and expecting to be 'in position' at almost any minute. Most – most are happy. We did get an amazing welcome when we arrived. All the people turned out and gave us any manner of things: beer, wine, hot coffee, cigars, baccy, tinned meat, chocolate, handshakes. I got three kisses (not the kind you need worry about) as we went through. The other battalion arrived on Sunday and is already in the trenches. You know how bad my French is . . . well, I can talk some Flemish already!

We didn't get off from Southampton till a.m. and I worked until I nearly dropped loading the cargo. The moon was shining very bright. I got some sleep on deck propped against some pipes and was very snug. Our food is biscuits and bully beef. The sea was as smooth as a billiard table, and part of the way we were escorted by English torpedo-boat destroyers and met by French ones.

When we entrained for Belgium we were eight men in each carriage, so had to sleep sitting straight up. A young officer called Fletcher would fall on to me! We are awfully pleased to get a chance of fighting before Kitchener's army and in an important place, too.

On our way we saw villages with beautiful cottages – we'll have one next year! – well-fed cattle, rich soil, cobbled roads, huge churches and dignified shops. Some of these were in haze as dawn came up. How long will it last like this? At least I feel I may be of some use. They say there are lots of spies. The story is going round of an old fat woman selling choc-olates; she proved to be a German soldier.

I have some Belloc poems and two books to read: Thomas Hardy, *Tess of the D'Urbervilles*, and Masefield's *Multitude and Solitude*. Sometimes I feel like Masefield's 'Dauber'. Did I tell you about the poem? It concerns an artist who is frustrated because he has the true urge to write but lacks the technical gifts. How are you enjoying Mrs Rice's *Mr Opp*?

There are some very beautiful children in Belgium. Perhaps we will be lucky. I love you so much.

Your Wilfred

X X X X X X

11th Oct.

Darling Wilfred,

Things at first seemed far worse than I feared and my nerves were terribly on edge. Then I thought of you as I sat in front of a warm fire and was ashamed. But I don't want to think *too* much of your condition because it upsets me and I am trying to keep cheerful. If I look miserable no one stops pestering me here.

I miss you dreadfully. Although I lead my usually lazy life I am strangely tired out, probably with longing to be with you. I jump when the door knocks. When mother goes on a bit I take my thoughts away and build a house for us in Suffolk or Kent. I often think how happy we shall be because we've been through so much already and I have none of the fears of not knowing my husband. Funny word, isn't it? I don't think I've used it to you before.

I'm trying to learn all I can about ballet and tapestries so that I know something you do not. That will be your fault for encouraging me to learn! And when you're home – please make it *soon* – I shall read to you as you like to lie back with your pipe, and eyes closed. No facetious comments will be allowed.

I wish I could sit writing letters and reading yours all day but I force myself to go for walks with Victoria and busy myself with small jobs. It has the advantage of stopping self-indulgence, which I think you would approve of. At least that is what I tell myself.

Saffron and Jooey send their own best wishes to you. I went round to see Saffron and talked to your parents for a while.

They were very keen to know of anything I had heard from you; they're terribly proud of you, Wilfred, and the only thing you ever did wrong in their eyes was to marry your Eileen. Do be terribly careful. I know you won't listen but please PLEASE. I ask this because I love you.

Eileen

14th Oct. 1914

Darling Eileen,

We are now in the convent which accommodates our entire strength. It was a three and a half mile march to get here – how precise one becomes when one marches every step! The convent sounds quite grand and indeed the outside looks like a rather inferior unfinished Cambridge court. In the inside such comparisons are at an end! There is no water laid on, no light, no method of heating or drying clothes. There is no furniture to sit on and think of you and there are no extra rations to fill the hole in my stomach. The only bright spot was the news that a rum ration begins tomorrow. The men seem cheery enough.

The weather has been very wet and we have been out in it all day digging trenches and organising artillery formation. We are, however, considered most efficient and ready because we are to leave on the 16th.

I've thought very hard about this and have decided to tell you the truth. Although the men think me exceptionally hard and tough, I feel very frightened at the idea of battle. A feeling of coldness came over me as I heard that aeroplanes are being shelled only 20 miles away.

As I work or march I carry my picture of you; you walk with me every step. Although I cannot talk to the men of my fears I am telling you. Before I came out here I thought it was a grand opportunity and we should spare no effort. I hope I live up to that.

How are Saffron and Jooey? They must be enjoying those walks with you. Do they miss me?

Don't hold back from me. Tell me all your thoughts in whatever form they come.

Your lover, Wilfred

Oct. 18th

Darling Eileen,

Three days ago we had a long slog. The roads were pavée almost all the way in our 17½ miles march. And it rained! Despite all this the men seem very much on their mettle and not a single one fell out of column. The next day's march was only eleven miles but with bruised feet it seemed longer. We spent the night very close to the place where the Artists and Honourable Artillery Company are in billets. We saw the remnants of another Brigade coming out of action and it was a sobering sight. Yesterday we moved one step nearer Ploegsteert and the firing line. This time the march was in a thunderstorm. What else is there left for the elements to do? It is now up to the human race to act.

A Brigadier-General visited us today and addressed the officers and outlined the scheme of training. We are mostly to be concerned with trench training and when not actually in line we will have 'fatigues' of all kinds to do. The London

Fatigues! Tonight we leave – for the trenches via Ploegsteert. You can imagine the jokes the place attracts. Plug this and plug that. I hope it continues that way. I am feeling much better now, having little difficulty in undergoing the routine and marvellously helped by your letters. When extra work is being given us it is called having the 'dripping swung' on us, and when the dripping is swung on us it is your letters that warm up my cold hands. When the mail comes in we all dash. Sometimes the letters are late because they're a little slack in forwarding them.

My darling, at least I have someone on whom I can and will lavish all my devotion and love.

In this strange world I hold on to you. Despite rumours to the contrary I love you more than ever! Of course you can read to me with that marvellous beautiful voice.

Wilfred

29th Oct.

Darling Wilfred,

It is quite mild today so I've been for a walk, and thought about the times we spent over the last two summers doing the same thing. I remember the lovely lilac smells that came on the breeze on those paths and you would hold my hand and tell me about things we saw in the hedgerows. What a lucky girl to be asked to dance at the Ball!

I wish I knew more about flowers because I could then decide whether the ones I've noticed are rare or not. I must know more about everything. It will stop me becoming mor- bid about what may be happening to you. I'm afraid I pore over *The Times* every day with dread that I will find your name in the lists of injured. (I wouldn't have told you this but you insisted that I told you everything.) Victoria has been much kinder recently and I really think she is beginning to understand my feelings a bit better. This may be because some of her young men have volunteered in the last few days and you are now in good company. Isn't it sad how we only grasp a thing fully when we stand to lose something? This morning she looked across the table with obvious affection at my daily delight in reading your letter. (If a new one does not arrive I read an earlier one again, probably for the hundredth time.) A letterless day is difficult to bear but fortunately there are few.

(Later) I feel happy and light-headed now, so different from the morning when I woke up crying. Silly girl! I'm still reading Arnold Bennett but can't think of anything to say about it yet, unlike those brilliant Cambridge men. I'm enjoying it very much and delighted it is only one book in a series. You will simply have to sit and listen to me telling you about it. You aren't laughing at me, are you?

All my tender love to Wilfred,
Your Eileen

10th Nov. 1914

Darling Eileen,

This place is a long way from the Turkey Trot and the Wusky Woozle. Shirley Kellogg would not walk any joy plank out here. The nights are cold and can be very lonely. The days are full of repetitive jobs – and nor is fifteen rounds rapid much fun.

I've been trying to think back to the feelings and thoughts I had in August and early September and in the first weeks of this year. Four months ago I was in the hospital, getting very heated and feeling so much could be done for all people. You remember how angry and ashamed I was at some of the housemen's indifference to ordinary people and the mistakes by our senior surgeons. How worried I was! I thought I could do better.

And now, darling, what do I feel in Belgium now? The Germans are just across there and today Wilkinson died. It is no dream – we are unseen by each other but shells and bullets join us. It is bleak and may it soon be over. My mind, even as I work to drop, is full of you and my studies. I walk by the Thames with you. I take you to bed in a small little home in the country. I love you and do not feel guilt.

In the mornings we will talk seriously about things. Do you remember the talks about the demonstration of the Suffrage Societies in Hyde Park? How amused you were that I felt you should be more concerned about these women, and might even feel yourself represented by them. You said, 'I'm free as long as I have you.'

How far away suffragettes seem; there are no women here. Everyone is equal in a trench when bullets fly and shells drop. No one is a chief surgeon, no one is an ordinary man. We are all more vulnerable than we ever think. So do be prepared.

You are always in my heart,

Your Wilfred x x x x

Ploegsteert

18th Nov.

Eileen, my darling,

Thank you so much for your letters, from the bottom of my heart. I've been trying to recover my mood before writing this because the events here today have been sickening. But as soon as the cry 'Mail Up' goes round I charge off to collect, hopefully, yours – and I'm usually lucky and when I'm not I blame Boulogne, the port they all come through. Not that this is fair because lately the mail has been very efficient indeed.

I am leaning up against the wall of a barn, such a nice old barn too. It was never meant to see such days as today. Now it is so weird because I can hear myself breathing. We have really been up against it today so I treasure these moments of escape. After a few weeks of this I am already thinking of the meaning of life! How different from the abstract discussion at Trinity Theological meetings!

If we have any children we must teach them about the horrors of this war, and *all* killing. You might think I should be the first to learn this lesson after my behaviour a few months ago. But we all grow up misled by the poetry of battle. I have been having a very quiet time here compared with some other areas where the fighting is unceasing but I have already seen men nerve-racked by explosions and people dead, hit by bullets or flying pieces of rubble. To a child it is a game with flags and beautiful uniforms. I remember I always had a pre-dilection for bright colours and martial uniforms and it took me a long time to get over my chagrin when the British changed to khaki from red tunics in the Boer War. And I was still a child in July and would not listen. Today, however, I met a young officer who talked about a burst of fire as a 'lovely scrap' and I was given a jolt. After six weeks of this they can still talk like that.

I'm sorry to hear you are often unhappy and that Mrs Thumper is still not being friendly in the best sense. When I come back we must be firm and make our lives ourselves. I have never been sufficiently outspoken. But I'm glad you're not doing anything rash because it would only make things worse. Please send me another photograph and I can carry it with me . . . Forget about your ideas of the 'clever Cambridge crowd'. I didn't live a bit until meeting you. What good is cleverness out here? I want to be a doctor, a surgeon and I want to be happy with you.

Please give my regards to all yours. Good news about Victoria.

All my love to you, Your Wilfred

30 Nov. 1914

Darling Eileen,

I think this business will last longer than was expected in August and is on a bigger scale. You probably know more about it from *The Times* and *Daily Mail* than we know out here.

Thank you for your wonderful letter. We all get very wild when the mail arrives and rush for letters. The men vanish like moles with them. In the evenings I sit with a glass of local wine (which is excellent) and read yours through and through.

I really spoil myself but I am sad to hear the atmosphere in London is strained. Darkened streets, searchlights and casualty lists. What are they saying and thinking at home? How awful for you! I hope you are not too depressed.

We take turns to spend the night in trenches. Sometimes one bumps into somebody and gets awfully frightened. The nights are very black. I can't think how I've been alive so long without knowing the blackness of night – one doesn't sleep outside in Kensington! London was very much in my thoughts tonight because some of the men have been coming up with songs and this is how one of them goes:

> Where are the lads of the village tonight?
> Where are the lads we know?
> In Piccadilly? In Leicester Square?
> No! Not there! No! Not there!
> They're taking a trip on the Continent
> With their rifles and their bayonets bright
> Facing danger gladly, where they're needed badly
> That's where they are tonight!

Not ragtime but it cheers me up, especially when I feel like grabbing my hat and bolting.

I get up at six-thirty to serve the rum ration. This is a fairly quiet part of the line although I can hear the guns. The shells start with a dull bang and go overhead like a whistling express train. But I have been quite safe. The trenches are called Regent Street, Piccadilly, The Strand, Hyde Park Corner. Quite like home.

I remember every minute of those walks we had in the summer with Saffron and Jooey. Do you remember how angry I got when Jooey followed Saffron after a rabbit? Jooey swimming with his little hairy paws trying to keep up! I feel ashamed now of how I used to show off about the big chub I caught with Dutch cheese. And why was I so shy? Perhaps the dogs won't tell anything about us.

It's Sunday today. Five months ago on Sundays you came over to my home and, if it was wet, we went into the billiard room where I tried to make you a player. And I got so impatient when you missed!

All my love to you,
Wilfred

3rd Dec. 1914
Ploegsteert

My darling Eileen,

Your letter was read and read again before I sat down this evening. It was waiting for me as I came in from the edge of the wood and it cheered me more than the sun this morning. Yes, with your letters there are beautiful natural things in Ploegsteert.

I cannot tell you how glad I am you are getting on better at home. Perhaps that is one good thing to come out of our separation, darling. I have your photos to look at when I feel low. Yesterday we lost two men, only half an hour after we had heard of the sinking of two more merchant vessels off Havre. We feel even less safe now.

On my last visit to the town the market was empty. There was no bread and the local people talk wildly about spies. Day by day we can see morale lowering but I try not to join in the weary, gloomy, talk. Instead I make a conscious effort to think of you and me, our future, when there will be no bullets and no hostile families. So my name is no longer prohibited in the Stenhouse rooms?

When I look across the trench I sometimes think of Keats' words:

'So the two brothers and their murdered man

Rode past fair Florence.'

Or is 'my number up', in the words they use here.

Forgive this letter. I love you. I'll write at greater length next time.

Wilfred

6th December

Darling Wilfred,

It is a damp, dreary old December day but your news has thrilled me. You seemed much more like Wilfred in your last letter. I was a little perturbed by some of the recent ones but you seem back to your lively ways. You have so much strength and discipline, haven't you? I can see you there with your pipe puffing or reading or cheering up the men in your positive manner. Shall I send you some more books? I haven't any more photographs I'm afraid, darling, but I will try to arrange some.

You asked about the atmosphere at home. Well, I am now less anxious and I think this has affected everyone for the better. You have helped me care a little less about 'doing the right thing' and even when Guy Wilson was here and being very depressing about the War, I managed to keep cheerful and not run out and cry. His rather stiff manner was such a contrast to your quiet personal letters. The *Morning Post* is full of grand and pompous articles and letters. They ought to publish yours, not that they have a chance.

Can I tell you something silly? When I lie in bed reading your words I want to run down the street shouting at the top of my voice 'My Wilfred says this . . . my Wilfred says that. . . .' 'But how do you know he's right?' someone calls from a window. 'Because I'm his little wifey and I say so.' How childish I am and I'm blushing as I write that. I must stop now. You'll be saying 'she's dangerously happy'. I am. You're so balanced and I love that, too.

Please be very careful and tell me everything.

All love to you,
Eileen

8th December

Darling Eileen,

Bless you for your letters. It has been a tough day so far. This morning I gave instructions to some men about patrolling, stalking and crawling. But it wasn't the kind of day one wants to practise that kind of thing so I had to be firm with them. The clouds are low and heavy – as is the smell here!

The guns have been sounding less threatening and one sleeps so much better. Last night Osbert Davidson and I drank a bottle of wine while he told me about his cricket for Sussex. Before long he was describing his best innings and the clouds rolled away from his eyes. It was wonderful to see someone so happy simply recollecting a game. He finished up turning on to his side and saying 'Thanks, Wilfred.' All I did was listen.

I am not against the kind of hard work we did today but I wonder how our parts fit into the overall plan, if there is one. I suppose the people who are moving the troops round know what they are doing but since we arrived nearly ten weeks ago I have never heard a convincing explanation of the set-up. This place is very like a real distorted dream if you understand. It is like a large, messy muddy envelope with ladders there to drop you down into the slit. Mounds of earth are piled high all around us. We are in a war but don't have the feeling of being in any particular country. The nearby village is rapidly losing its normal way of life and so there is less point in trying to get there for a few hours. The only people who even know the enemy are 'there', out there, for sure, are the people who have been killed or wounded. No, that is stupid.

In a sense you are here with me. As I stamp up and down trying to keep warm or cursing my luck when I have to stand in for someone, I find I stop complaining to myself when I think of you. So you, too, are helping maintain discipline! People call me 'Wiry Willett'. If only they knew how clammy my hands were when there's danger and how my ribs bang when there's trouble.

You'll never see this place and I'm glad of that. I'll write again tomorrow.

Your lover,
Wilfred

Dec. 9th.

Darling Eileen,

Ploegsteert. Have I ever lived anywhere else? Yes, of course, and yet it seems so long ago. The LRB, The Fatigue Fifth, has been remaking a support line in the wood, named Bunhill Row. The weather could not have been worse and the ground is impossible. The river flowed over and badly flooded our trenches. Too much dirty water up our legs. Once a week we can escape back to the Brewery, the Battalion Bath-house, and have a wash. It is very good for one to realise how much one takes basic things for granted. To wash in clean water may seem a simple matter in Ashburn Place; in Ploegsteert it is like going to the theatre.

Our quota of work has helped to transform P wood. Despite the weather we can now walk across most of it. The corduroy no longer stops at the worst parts. Rations can come through at a reasonable pace as long as they keep to the boards. As the Senior Chaplain said, 'Everything in the garden is as near lovely as can be.' You would like him because he's very amusing and keeps us cheerful.

The village has been shelled to pieces and every house has a hole in it. As I lunched with Walsh and Bushby and five company officers today – fresh fish and potatoes, fruit, cheese and coffee – I found it hard to believe a war was on. Then a shell burst and knocked over someone's vin ordinaire!

I have not yet seen a German – but there are periscopes and peepholes further along, from which point the Germans are only forty yards away. Most of all I would like to change my boots every day. And my next pleasure would be rhubarb tart and cream. Some men get hampers sent from Harrods with all manner of delicacies.

Why not come over in one? I'll look after you.

Your love,
Wilfred

21 Holland Villas Road
Kensington
20th January, 1915

Dear Mr Wright,

Thank you for your letter and kind enquiries about my son, Wilfred. He was, I regret to say, shot through the left side of the head on the 13th ulto. and last Friday he was brought over and is at present under Mr Worthington's care at 49 Belgrave Square, part of which house Lord Aberdovey has kindly placed at the disposal of the authorities of King Edward VI Hospital.

It is with the greatest regret that I have to say that Sir Roger Parsons and the other doctors who have seen him say that he will never be able to continue his studies, and that as a rule in similar injuries the patient does not recover from the paralysis but we are living in the hope that his case may prove the exception.

His mother read your letter to Wilfred and he managed to say 'Good sort. Kind. Thank him.'

Please accept my wife's and my thanks,

With kind regards,
Yours sincerely,
T H Willett

By the thirteenth of December the first Christmas mail had begun to arrive along with embossed tin boxes from Princess Mary containing a pipe and extra tobacco. As Wilfred's platoon was specially detailed for trench clearing the Christmas spirit helped them bale out and rivet waterlogged trenches. They were exceptionally wearing days because pointless: the sides tended to fall back in. This provided the challenge Wilfred had been wanting; if the odds seemed insurmountable he rushed about urging and cajoling but mostly doing three men's labour. From his example the others attacked their jobs, even managing to be lively and high-spirited. He forced himself to think of Eileen.

How much chance had he of spending Christmas with Eileen? Would he soon – not too soon but not too long – be walking along the embankment telling her of his day in the hospital, and his plans when he was qualified? The thought quickened and panicked his feelings; what did she look like, feel like? He forced his mind through a painful run of details. What is the exact colour of her hair? Think. Right. The look in her eyes? Right. The feel of her hands, the side of her breasts, the back of her shoulders, the softness of her arms, the way she walks? The outline of her spine? Right. Now her voice. Warm, slow, yes he had it. He had all of her. Nobody, thought Wilfred, feels as I feel. In the absolute secrecy of his heart he held her, self-sufficient; he had confided in no one in the past and would not now.

Two men were suddenly hit. A sergeant shouted across to him because he was known as a 'doctor', and Wilfred scrambled about thirty yards to help. He always carried morphia in his pockets for these occasions and usually managed 'to do them up' as best he could. He found he quickly slipped into his professional frame of mind – indeed with an ease that later troubled him. As he stood in his trench having a quiet pipe in the mornings he felt some fear for his spirit, a fear more intense than the physical cringing experienced when he heard the slow whine of small shells and the wasp-'ping' of bullets.

Was he becoming callous after only a few deaths? Was he already toughening into 'a theatre of war, that's all it is, like a theatre in the hospital'? Would he feel this if he wasn't in a quiet area on the edge of the wood? Was he hoping to make a name for himself by his psychological toughness, a name he would never make in peace or if more wholeheartedly involved in the action? While staunching the blood and comforting the men Wilfred felt cool and quiet inside, loving his difficult task and only wishing it was his fortune to walk back with them to continue treatment.

When he had seen them on their way, one of them shrieking, one of them murmuring thanks, Wilfred crouched right down and squelching and very hot made ground back to his platoon. When he got there the platoon sergeant was waiting and whispered, 'Moore's hit, sir, he's rolled down the other side of the parapet.' Wilfred jumped up and looked.

'I shouldn't stand there, sir, if I was you, you're right out in the open.' Wilfred leapt across the trench, followed by the sergeant, and knelt down by Moore. Lifting his head Wilfred peered round – all was still and quiet – and down on to the man. His leg was quite badly damaged, bone and trousers mixed, blood seeping into his boots, Wilfred asked him about the pain and grasped that he could move his back and the other leg. What was the best way to get him down without risking any further casualty? Wilfred straightened to see how many men were close enough to help without endangering themselves. He was pitched on to his shoulder and over on to his side.

The sergeant looked down at Wilfred, whose right arm was still touching Moore in a reassuring pose. Wilfred's face was bleary and irritable; he turned and tried to crawl down the slope; blood pumped out of his head and down the side of his nose. There was a hole in the back of his skull like a half-eaten red egg. The sergeant wormed down on his stomach and pulled first Moore and then Wilfred into the trench; helping hands levered them and broke their slumping fall.

Although he felt no pain, at least no more than being trodden on in a rugger match, Wilfred could not speak or utter a sound. He was lifted, pulled, placed and talked to by familiar faces, all trying to comfort and communicate. Try as he might he could do nothing beyond lift his right arm a fraction in token acknowledgment; he wanted to thank them and yet experienced a deep sense of relief that he would no longer have to prove his selfless efficiency. He knew he would soon be with Eileen again, in her arms and talking of their feelings. Why were the faces so serious? Yes, that was Thompson leaning over, soaking up a little pool which was making his left eye sticky, and then there was – who was that? – opening a dressing. They were so helpful, heads filling the greyness, breathing on to him. He would soon be home.

Wilfred realised the base of his skull was cracked, his brain damaged, he thought it was the Broca's and Rolandic areas. He heard the men talking as they carried him, jogging and jerking through trench after trench. Thompson wiped clear some scattered brain substance which was oozing out behind Wilfred's ear, and briefly other faces passed, mouths opening with an encouraging comment. Wilfred tried to smile recognition to these friends – he had talked to Thompson only the other day about reactions to death and injury – because he was glad they were there. But the smiles wouldn't come; this exasperated him because he did not want a sentimental farewell; whether he lived or died he did not want there to be any morbid emotions. 'Of course,' Wilfred said to himself, 'I haven't the slightest intention of dying. There'll be no more blue fingers and wet feet for a while, and perhaps the war'll be over by the time I'm fit again . . . Eileen's hands, no more damp, sticky mackintoshes. . . .'

By the time they had bumped Wilfred the final two hundred yards he had vomited on himself. Although he had tried to tell them they seemed unconcerned, moving up the slope and into a barn which was being used as a relief hospital. Very cold and increasingly low in mood he decided to brush away the caked sick from his throat and shirt, but he found he could not locate the spot; he tried to focus on the trees outside the door but they were flickering in the half-light. And did it really matter about the trees, did it really matter, because they were all swaying happily, they were all pulling together towards him?

An Anglican and a Catholic priest came in quietly and knelt one on each side of his head, the Anglican with eyes closed next to the hard brown blood, the Catholic looking at the wet, fresh wound.

For the next ten hours no decision was taken about Wilfred's move. Everyone expected him to die. By the time he was taken back to the large hospital at Boulogne he was in a coma and knew nothing of the long journey; he simply gave up the struggle to talk and fell back into warmth, unaware of his condition beyond the cursory self-diagnosis immediately after he was hit. In brief moments of clarity he realised he was paralysed on the right side because that was why no one tried to talk to him from there – they all came to him on the left.

Wilfred noticed the texture of the blankets, how different from those at the woodman's hut. These were prickly and coarse, without the flannelly touch of those intimate ones. And the food – he tasted it and even found some words to match the flavour, words his mind was pleased with but that his mouth could not form. Nevertheless he was encouraged by these life signs; he was determined to ask the nurse to ask the surgeon . . . she merely 'shushed' his efforts at waving and he was soon asleep, brilliant black-red flashes behind his eyelids.

CHAPTER FIVE

WILFRED AND EILEEN

Eileen had received no letter from Wilfred since one dated December 11th and was seriously upset; the mail had been so reliable up till then. After three days she called on the Willetts to find out if they had any more. They had heard nothing either and were a little concerned, too, but then their letters were not quite so frequent. On the fifth morning of waiting Eileen was sure that there had been a terrible disaster and went to the Brigade headquarters. It was their 'first' wedding anniversary and Wilfred would never have forgotten to write for that. No, they unfortunately did not know anything beyond what she knew although the weekly bulletin might have some additional information and when it came in they would be sure to let her know anything relevant. Yes, they would certainly check up and see if there had been any errors or omissions in the printed lists.

But none of this placated Eileen. He was hers, not the Army's, not the LRB's. 'Eileen, you must try to be patient. You know your father is doing all he can to find out about Wilfred.'

'But there's no reaction. I've written to them twice; I've written to Wilfred; I've made telephone calls; they simply say I must wait for the official news. Well, I won't.'

'Everyone has to wait, dear. Thousands of people are going through this most distressing experience along with you.'

'I don't care about the thousands of people. I don't know them and I don't want to. Something dreadful has happened to Wilfred and no one will tell me.'

Eileen had been crying in her bed before breakfast and as the tears were coming again she left the table and went to her room. There she controlled herself, gathered her things together for a walk in the cold air, and moved down the back stairs. She could hear the servants discussing the arrangements for Christmas as she slipped outside through the tradesman's entrance. There was going to be an end to this nonsense; she had never before encountered official silence and blocking, although Wilfred had told her of such maddening things working their insidious, apparently 'necessary' way into every department of Hospital life.

Eileen felt it was even worse for her. This was not a matter of career moves or politics – it was life and death; Wilfred's! The streets were full of shoppers as if it was any other Christmas. How could they shop so unconcernedly when such things were happening? There might be no war on for the inane way they carried on with their boxes and fancy wrappings. She refused to return the smile to the newspaper-man who sold her a *Morning Post*; what was the point of smiling? As Wilfred's name was not in the casualty lists again, nor mentioned in the communiqués, she looked up the Whitehall address of the War Office. But they'll try to brush me off, she thought; very well, let them try. She found herself practising a haughty don't-give-me-that as she took a taxicab; now this is my husband we are talking about; yes, it may surprise you but it is, and I'd be grateful to be treated as such and not like a little girl. No need for smiles, let's have no endearing comforts – simply where is he at this moment?

As she asked for attention she practised an interior voice, trying to sound hard. But mustn't overdo it. Not that the first man could have taken it; he was nice to the point of timid. His face was pale and strained, possibly from many such inter-views; the floor was highly polished and clipped his feet as he moved around; a dark rug changed the tone when he paused there. Hurriedly and without a trace of her intended panache Eileen told her worries and the facts. How vulnerable she sounded!

'Right, Mrs Willett, isn't it? Right, I'll see what I can do. I won't keep you a minute longer than I need. The LRB? Lieut. W L Willett, Ploegsteert, Belgium. Posted October you say? Now, you last heard from him in a letter of December . . .'

'That's correct.'

The man left. Others came in and out at varying intervals without acknowledging Eileen, collecting files, looking at sheets of paper on the desk, humming mechanically. Even with their eyes shut they would have avoided bumping into the bulky furniture in that crowded room. Why were people so afraid of making contact with her, why not lean over to her and . . . no, no, she did not want that. She had come for the plain facts, like the plain facts about the wards that Wilfred wanted to tell. The man returned.

'Please come this way, Mrs Willett.'

She followed along the corridors to a somewhat larger but similar room. The new official was also courteous but more confident.

'I am sorry about all this. Do sit down. In fact we didn't hear until last night, Mrs Willett, that your husband was wounded on December 13th in the trenches at Ploegsteert. It seems the delay was because the doctors did not want to give information until they had decided whether to keep your husband in France or send him back to England. He is, however, still in France, at our base hospital in Boulogne. He has been there at least three days and is under close observation.'

'Oh how awful, how . . . why, why didn't they tell me straight away? On the 13th? I could have written to him, sent him things.'

'Quite, but that's all I know . . . this news would normally be in the papers the very next day so I expect there was a special reason. You'll appreciate the complex situation with thousands of men involved every day, often under conditions of extreme difficulty, and they don't like to release information until they are very sure of their facts. From our point of view the Belgian frontier has been particularly fraught with communication problems.'

Eileen was struggling with her grief. His words missed her; she saw Wilfred floundering in a miasma, in putrid vapours, calling to her and no one telling her he was calling. He tried to rise out of the trench to grab her hand but she was sitting by the fire talking to Victoria. Shivering she pulled her coat tighter and stood up.

'Thank you for telling me. Now I know, at least I know.'

'If there's anything I can do please let me know, anything at all, please do.'

'Yes, there is. Where can I obtain a passport?'

He told her; his face sharpened and the generalised understanding passed from his eyes.

'It is not permitted, of course, for civilians to cross to France at the present time. The war regulations are quite specific on that. And it is Christmas also.'

'Thank you,' she said, and left.

To hell with Christmas! She scurried along through the crisp air, breathing out firmly with new energy. Since 'being told' she had been talking to Wilfred in her mind, and the interior dialogue strengthened every step she took. He would soon be convalescing in her bedroom at her home, she would arrange it, and no one from either family would be able to visit without her permission. She would see him well; at last this was a private matter between the two of them.

* * *

By any standards it proved to be a splendid Christmas dinner at the Stenhouses and well worth a special word of thanks to the cook and the kitchen generally. If anything they had put that little bit extra in, the war being on and poor Miss Eileen. All over London too, extra little bits were being done to make this Christmas one never to forget; there may be a war on, many of the men may be away, the hopes that it would be over by now may have been a trifle premature, there was no snow it was true, but it *was* Christmas. Each exquisite course took Eileen back eighteen months to Cambridge and the only formal dinner she had ever enjoyed; and not because she really did spend it with Wilfred. But he was *there*, he was at the table; if only that were the case now. She remembered the candles and the flickering lights and the gay nonsense talked across the girls and that rather shy man she had seen on the bank in the afternoon, the one they enjoyed teasing. Wilfred he was called. She had caught his eye, he rather curiously caught hers. The confident banter of the group had slightly put her off at first but they were only weeks away from the City, or the Law or some kind of discipline; it was their last chance. If they'd known they were only eighteen months from this war then the festivities would have been even wilder. Wilfred, why did you volunteer? If only you hadn't, but you did, you would, wouldn't you?

'A little more wine, Eileen dear?'

'Yes, thank you.'

'I'm so glad you're enjoying it.'

She had tried very hard and was not going to fall at the last hurdle. No one must sense anything was wrong. Only at the appropriate hour did she move towards the door, turn, excuse herself as sweetly as possible and go upstairs. In the haven of her own room she opened the third drawer from the top of her little mahogany cabinet and unfolded a large, strong piece of white paper. It crackled as it opened. It read –

○ ○ ○ ○ ○ ○ ○ ○

'We, Sir Edward Grey, a Baronet of the United Kingdom of Great Britain and Ireland, Knight of the Most Noble Order of the Garter, a Member of His Britannic Majesty's Most Honourable Privy Council, a Member of Parliament, His Majesty's Principal Secretary of State for Foreign Affairs, Request and require in the Name of His Majesty, all those whom it may concern to allow

Mrs Eileen Estelle Josephine Willett,

British Subject, travelling to France

to pass freely without let or hindrance and to afford her every assistance and protection of which she may stand in need. Given at the Foreign Office, London, December 22nd, 1914.

Age of Bearer, 22 years.

Profession of bearer, Nil

Signature of bearer. . . .'

From the War Office Eileen had rushed to the Foreign Office where she was politely told she could not see the Secretary of State nor indeed any other secretary, but if she called at ten o'clock the next morning she could put her case for a special passport in the appropriate quarter. Such things, then, *were* allowed.

On her return journey home she saw two courses of action open: to consult her father, who knew a number of influential people who might know the best person to approach for such a dispensation, or to go on alone. By the time she arrived in Ashburn Place she had made her decision and was as resolute as she had been just over a year ago, whatever the repercussions, to marry a man 'slightly beneath her' in a Registry Office. Part of it, of course, was distaste for and fear of the row that would inevitably occur when she raised the issue. There would be a refusal to 'consider it' and then would come the endless watching and conspiratorial chats to ensure that she did 'nothing silly'. She could tell someone, but whom could she trust? With anyone else there was sure to be a slip-up. She would trust herself and keeping it to herself would be one of the few pleasures she could think of at this ghastly time. As it turned out Eileen had quite enough trouble explaining away where she had been for two and a half hours that morning to be sure she had made the right decision in keeping secret her attempt at the Foreign Office.

Something curious was happening to Eileen. She noticed it that night in her face. She was not by nature self-analytical and no one's habits and instincts could have been further from narcissism; sometimes she dressed if anything rather too casually, people thought, without sufficient attention to detail and straightness of hemline – even safety pins had been seen in her dress. But as she looked into the mirror she was caught and held by something dignified, tenacious, almost wilful in the eyes. Her mouth was set. This most adaptable and sensitive girl was revealing the firmness which perhaps had attracted Wilfred that night in Cambridge.

It was in this mood that Eileen met the official in the Foreign Office. She had to wait for the exact moment of appointed time, noticing in the meanwhile that everything seemed more cushioned than at the War Office. Here everyone was sedately going about his business; hectic it may have felt, it may have been in the very perfection of confusion, but it looked sedate. Suddenly she was talking across the table, coherently giving her reasons for the visit. Behind the man's well-groomed head the rain lashed impetuously on the window. To justify her course Eileen decided on a personal move, more personal than she had ever intended:

'If your wife was lying very ill or possibly dying in Boulogne and you felt you could help and no one else seemed to care would you sit here and let the days pass?'

'I can see that, Mrs Willett, I can. Please go on.'

'Because, you see, I believe I can help my husband and I don't think anyone else can.'

She did not hurry on. She said no more. Unknown to Eileen there had been a stroke of luck in that office at four-thirty the previous evening; a young man had made a most convincing plea because his fiancée, a nurse on a short spell of duty in one of the base hospitals, was seriously ill with peritonitis. And try as he might, and without a trace of sympathy for any woman who dashed all over the place on her own in a war situation, the official could see no difference in the cases, except that this woman furthermore was married, respectable and palpably well enough off to travel comfortably.

He authorised the passport and told Eileen to call at three the following afternoon by which time it would be ready and countersigned by the French Consul General in London. Eileen had won her rights, and in an earnest outburst of gratitude unsettled the man.

And there as she folded it away, was her firm signature at the bottom and the signature of Monsieur Gérard Cernay.

Aptly a French sentence completed her English passport: '*De bon vouloir servir le roy*'. For the first time in ten days she settled down to read Arnold Bennett.

* * *

Boulogne seemed far less warlike than Dover. Both were full of troops and mailbags but the Dover patrols and mine-sweepers moved ceaselessly up and down; when Eileen arrived in France she felt sure she was going to hear the guns. She had no sure grasp of 'The Front'. It was dark as she came down the gangplank and the harbour lights were flickering fitfully on the water. A young man, a war correspondent, had fallen into conversation with her over the last part of the voyage and had promised to find out where the military hospital was. While he went off Eileen smelt and tasted the oil and herring on the breeze; even if it was not a happy reason to cross the Channel, it was the first time since her finishing school in Switzerland; even alone and in December, perhaps because she was alone and it was December, it was an adventure. It was something she would never have dreamed of doing before she met Wilfred, and she was not even now sure how she had managed it.

'I think I know where it is. I am afraid my French is pretty ropey and it took me a while to find an Englishman. Would you believe it? The whole place is under British administration and control, and nothing but locals on view.'

'Isn't there anyone in an information room somewhere?'

'Probably, but I couldn't find the information room. Never

mind, I think we'll be all right. Are you ready for some walking? I'm sure there's no transport for civilians and if I were you I'd say as little as possible and just do it.'

'Oh good.' It was just the advice she wanted.

'What a girl! How did your family let you away? I can't see my father letting his beloved out of sight. You're not eloping are you?'

'Not exactly. But in a way. I'm trying to find my husband who's been wounded, and he's meant to be here.'

'How terrible! Sorry, didn't mean to joke about everything.'

'That's quite all right. You've been very kind.'

With the cathedral barely visible in the scanty light they walked on past hotels which had Red Cross signs hanging over their names, on through the fishermen's quarter, until they came to the hospital. Eileen turned to the young man and looked at him closely for the first time – he was fresh-faced and ginger-haired.

'Can I use your story,' he asked, 'if nothing better comes my way? Or is that a terrible cheek?'

'No it isn't, but I'd rather you didn't if you don't mind. Thank you so much for everything.'

An evidently overtired nurse was standing at the desk to know what Eileen wanted. Eileen explained who she was, and was very relieved to see a face hardened to unexpected and unwanted visitors soften as she spoke.

'And you've come across on your own; but that's extraordinary! It's really incredible! Do come in and we'll decide what we can do.'

She put her hand out and led Eileen into her rest room.

'Come on, you must be exhausted; quite apart from anything else it must have been perishing on the boat?'

'Not that I noticed; I wrapped up very tight!'

'And you'll be wanting to see your husband as soon as possible, but first a cup of tea while I try to get permission. We'll manage it, don't you worry.' She made the tea, pushing her hair from her face with steady, heavy gestures; she had the mechanical movements of someone who had been up for too many hours for too many days. No relaxing, exquisite Christmas for her, Eileen thought. With her back turned and her hands busied with the cups the nurse asked:

'So you know little more than the date your husband was wounded?'

'Nothing more. You know what it's like trying to find out information. One is treated like a child.'

'I do know. It drives one to distraction.'

'Well, how is he?'

'He's not at all well. He has a head wound and it has taken a long time to settle down. There's been a great deal of discussion between the doctors about whether to move him or to operate. One of the main issues is whether he can take the moving, and whether this place is the most suitable hospital to put things right.'

Eileen sat forward, her hands clenched white.

'Moved? Well, what does my husband think is best?'

'That's one of the problems, you see. I'm afraid he can't speak and is partially unconscious. I think you ought to know also that he can't move at present.'

'I suppose I've been expecting something on those lines,

only not quite as bad. I'm not sure exactly what I was dreading.' Eileen broke off to take the cup, and stared fixedly at a tea leaf steadily circling the rim. A couple of warm drops ran off her nose and she gulped into the tea.

'Nurse, what do you think will happen, do you think he will live?'

'I think so, yes, but you must ask the doctors. They'd go mad if they'd heard what I've said already. It's just that they're overworked, terribly so, and as I am not so busy I thought I'd better try to explain.'

Eileen was now weeping. The nurse took her cup and filled it again and left. What she had not dared tell Eileen was that the journey would be thought pointless by the senior doctor because he was sure Wilfred could not survive. There were, in any event, many patients who would probably benefit from surgery whereas this case was extremely difficult and likely to fail. A younger doctor, however, was not without hope; he thought further help in France was out of the question but that Wilfred would stand a chance if he could be got back to England without dying en route.

The door opened and the nurse re-entered.

'The doctors are busy at the moment but I can take you to see your husband. Now don't expect too much, will you? He's probably sleeping or at least rather hazy, and you mustn't worry him. You've had a hard day, too, remember.'

'I won't do anything silly, I promise.'

'And then you can come and eat with me. I'll arrange it.'

'No, no, I can't eat.'

'You can, you know.'

She set off along darkened corridors, beckoning Eileen to follow. My God, dear God, what do I do, Eileen thought; will he be the same, well, I know he won't be quite the same; if he was quite the same he wouldn't be here, would he; now, he won't look healthy, he'll look white and ill and it will be a shock, I know it will.

'Here is the ward. Now he's in the last bed along on the left-hand side. You will be quiet as you go through now, and be careful with the tables in the middle – the night lights are pretty dim. There should be a chair next to his bed; if not, take one from the other side of the ward.'

The ward held about twenty beds closely aligned with two long, rough tables running down the centre. An unventilated stench made Eileen gasp with disgust. She wavered, searching for an excuse to stop; she nearly walked deliberately into the table so that she could rub her leg and accustom herself further to the light. On the journey she had remembered in flashes all those moments she had most loved Wilfred, and so many warm pebbles had filled her mind. Now her brain questioned every illusion she had been creating about this moment. She felt terribly abandoned and defenceless as she stumbled on.

'Stop it, stop it,' she mumbled to herself. 'Stop being so weak. I'm sorry if I seem weak, Wilfred, I've tried so hard, darling, not to be weak.' She was nearly there and it would be over, she would *know*. She drew close to the last on the left, felt her way round the end with her fingers on the rough blanket and up to the head of the bed. She caught a glimpse of Wilfred's nose and the outline of his mouth.

His eyes were closed. With her right hand she drew up a chair and sat down with her face close to his. His hair was pushed back under the bandage which swathed his forehead. His face was leaner and taut with a pasty white shine. Taking his hand which lay outside the bedclothes she whispered and sobbed incoherently into the pillow near where his ear would be.

* * *

The younger doctor's hand was considerably strengthened by Eileen's arrival. With the care and assistance of a wife, the younger man argued, Willett might indeed make it back by boat to England; and negotiations for his return were quickly begun.

The last part of the journey by train from Dover was uncomfortable but uneventful compared with the nightmare crossing. The crossing nearly broke Eileen because Wilfred was so carelessly strapped on to the stretcher that he started to slip off between the boat and the jetty. Eileen screamed hysterically as he slid towards the water and was just caught. His face was grimacing; with irritation she thought at the time, but clearly he had been trying to draw attention to the strapping.

At Charing Cross the stretcher was carried through a narrow lane to the waiting ambulances while girls and other late workers stopped to look. Under the artificial lights from the station arc lamps their pale faces added to the tragic appeal, especially as it was now raining and the bearers were dressed in dark mackintoshes. Stretchers were of real interest; wheelchairs were two a penny.

In the first three days at the Belgrave Square annex many people came to see Wilfred. News had arrived from the doctors in Boulogne that an attempt would be made to transfer Lieut. Willett to this private temporary hospital; the news had also preceded Wilfred that he had been so seriously wounded while rescuing another wounded man. Masters from St Paul's, professors from the London, a bishop whom Wilfred had met a couple of times at Cambridge, and a few famous men he didn't know but who had made a point of visiting the wounded, all came. It was a flattering homage and he was wordlessly thankful.

All this was exceeded very shortly. Sir John French's next despatches were published and the families were overjoyed to see Wilfred's name mentioned for gallant and distinguished service. Eileen's eyes shone with pride as she heard her parents talk, and Mrs Thumper wrote to say she and Mr Willett felt the honour very much at this time. There was, however, a disappointment in store, for although he had been the only officer mentioned in the LRB, Wilfred did not receive a decoration. The adjutant did. This rankled in both households although Wilfred saw the justice of the award. It meant far more to a regular.

Even then there was no escaping from the war, it seemed, for in early February a letter of touching formality and irony was delivered to Wilfred's bed.

○ ○ ○ ○ ○ ○ ○ ○

Lealholme
Cliff Parade
Leigh-on-Sea

Dear Mr Willett,

Having reported myself on Friday at headquarters on termination of sick furlough, I was informed that you are now in hospital in London and am very glad to hear that you are making good progress. I am awfully sorry that you suffered so badly whilst attending to me, for which attention I shall feel ever grateful. Am very glad you were mentioned in Sir John French's last despatches, and congratulate you thereon. If possible I should very much like to see you before you return to France, so will call at the hospital one day this week.

As my wound is healing quite well now I am expecting to be sent to Haywards Heath with the 2nd Batt. very shortly.

With kindest regards,
Yours very sincerely,
E J Moore.

Wilfred, finding it very hard to respond, merely nodded acknowledgment of the man's gratitude. A little surprised, Eileen tucked the letter away. The wound in his head was not healing, he knew that, and still the damned specialist would not order an X-ray, even though Wilfred scratched the word on his slate. The whole place was a shambles, the apparatus was old – if a plate was taken it was sure to be too fogged to show anything. When Eileen complained she was advised to keep quiet: the hospital was under the patronage of a lady who, her father told her, was notoriously resentful of criticism. She was more worried that if she pushed too hard Wilfred might be sent home as hopeless.

The next morning, a fine one, Wilfred was wheeled to the open windows. He identified a chaffinch trying his quick song, a jolly sound. He was pleased he could recognise these things, but he was preoccupied with a growing fear. When nurses leant over to help him, when a tall slim girl swished through the room, even when Eileen touched his hand or put her face next to him on the pillow, he felt no desire. Late at night or early in the morning, in the half-aroused half-sleep, his mind did not play on her body; he could not recreate their love-making. The harder he tried the more upset he became. Should he tell her? He must. He shouldn't deceive her because it had been important. And it would be again. But *how* tell her?

Prostrate, he turned to the wall, blank. The colours and sounds outside grew less intense. The chaffinch flew away and shadows became mobile. A new noise was beating in his head, drumming the life, drumming the life out of him; he grabbed for the bell. His hand clattered the open window and a nurse scurried in.

By the time Eileen arrived Wilfred was in a violent and protracted Jacksonian convulsion, brought on, he knew, by the irritation caused by a cerebral abscess. She stood in horror of his epileptic state, his eyes on her as he writhed. Wilfred was acutely conscious of what was happening – he had learnt about this condition in his studies – and he could do nothing but watch Eileen watch him: if only he could step in, act, stop it.

⠀

Those trenches, his men. Ploegsteert, those hotel rooms, no no, the doctor's torch on a face in a badly pitched tent, huddled groups looking down as the sides flapped; an RAMC ambulance squelched up in the mud – 'Please, please' – he could hear Eileen begging to be let in, why was she here?

'Please, please, take him to the London Hospital. I don't *mind* what it costs, please.'

It was so simple, so simple it was amazing she hadn't thought of it before. Of course Mr Jenkins would help.

'I want my husband to be moved the moment he settles down.' Eileen ran to the office.

'Do I have to sign any papers? Of course I will.'

'This is most unusual, Mrs Willett, and I'm sure you're making a serious mistake. It will take a while to arrange.' The sister pointed to the spot where the signature was needed.

Eileen dashed back to Wilfred, two sisters now hurrying in behind her.

'Wilfred, I'm taking you to see Mr Jenkins. Just nod if you agree. It won't take an hour to get your things together. We'll explain when we get there.'

* * *

Wilfred was dreadfully shaken as they pulled into Whitechapel Road. Eileen's hand pressed on his cheek while she explained her plan: they were to ask for Mr Jenkins, no one else would do; if he was not in he was to be called and told one of his students needed his attention. Wilfred's name would do the trick, surely.

She helped carry Wilfred into the receiving room, where only months before he had seen everything from the doctor's point of view. His eyes flicked around the walls and chairs, picked up the details, quickly familiar. Eileen sat still, her hands firmly clasped in her lap, only reacting when a nurse or young doctor came in and out. Wilfred knew some of their faces but no one looked at him. One side of his face was sweating profusely. As Eileen wiped his forehead with her handkerchief Mr Jenkins entered, and briskly introduced himself to Eileen. His eyes were on Wilfred.

'I'm terribly sorry to come like this, doctor, but nothing was being done in Belgrave Square, and this morning he was in a kind of fit. I couldn't stand it any more.'

'Of course you've done the right thing, Mrs Willett. Now don't give it another thought, that's definite. Although the wards are full I think there's a spare student's room in which we can put him. He'll be looked after, I'll see to that, and you can pop and see him whenever you like. And so you're married, Willett, too! Two of us going in one year. Who'd have thought it!'

As he was talking Mr Jenkins was moving up to nurses gesturing them to help Wilfred into the small room along the corridor, worrying them through the door like a sheepdog.

'Now, Mrs Willett, please stay in the reception room while I have a word with him. We can find out a lot in no time and see the next move. He won't let me do anything without his permission, if I remember rightly.'

Eileen was too grateful. It was a different world. Overcome by his authority, by the general speed and efficiency, by Mr

Jenkins's direct strength, she slumped into a chair. For the first time since France she felt she was not entirely in the grip of events: a new adventure was beginning in which she was being helped to achieve her ends. The excitement in Wilfred's face proved she was right. It was a professional excitement, a thrill of respect in his eyes.

Mr Jenkins shut them all out.

'Well, Willett, what a heaven-sent opportunity for me! Now let's have a look. Obviously this looks a challenge for us!' And he started. Localised injury in otherwise healthy brain, fine prospect of exploration, a number of vital tests needed first, could succeed, would be a pleasure, at worst an interesting post-mortem, yes, there was a good chance if they thought it through, between them they would have a crack at it.

'Between us,' Wilfred thought. He motioned to write. Mr Jenkins took out some paper. Wilfred scrawled 'Must tell her truth.'

'Of course I will. Couldn't see much chance of getting away with less!' Wilfred raised his hand and Mr Jenkins was gone.

He led Eileen into his rooms, took her coat and explained his plan.

'It is possible in this test that your husband will suffer a further convulsion from another abscess which may keep on building up. But this is a situation where we can't leave well alone. He knows his problem, not in detail of course, but he realises there's no progress and there's little doubt he is low in morale. It'll be a long business and he'll become even lower. I've got excellent technicians here, and we'll try to take a close look at the splinters. The brain, as you may imagine, is extremely complicated but providing certain areas are unaffected – and there's a good chance they are – we can push on.'

'I want to stay if I can.'

'Where?'

'Here.'

'What, *now*, here?'

'If I could.'

'You can't stay tonight, I'm afraid, but I'll see what I can arrange. If you promise not to breathe a word to your husband about it – it's essential that he thinks you go home each night and that you behave as normally as possible – I'll see if we can put a mattress down. Not a word!'

The next morning the tests were begun. They were carried out with an alacrity and zest which suggested enthusiasm rather than last-minute urgency. Mr Jenkins studied the first X-ray plate, pinpointing the dead bone in the brain substance and pleased that although deeply embedded there were not too many splinters. Without even consulting his colleagues or asking for help he went to Wilfred.

'Good morning, Willett. Your wife's coming along this afternoon. Wonderful girl, isn't she, well done. Now, raise your hand if you can follow me. Good, that hand looks fine, it's the other side we've got to wake up a bit. What I'd like to do is this, difficult, mind, but still: open up the whole area where the trouble is and lift out those small pieces which are stopping you working on one side, and making the speech difficult. Probably playing around with your head doesn't appeal much but this needs to be on a decent scale or we could be in other problems. I expect you know all that. It would be a mistake to restrict the opening in the skull to a small one so I'm suggesting to you a decent job. Do you agree?'

Wilfred smiled his confidence and was disappointed not to have his smile returned. As he could not move one side of his face he seemed to be grimacing; smiling or grimacing, Mr Jenkins decided to go ahead.

'I'll see you later.'

* * *

Mr Jenkins needed Eileen's support and yet wanted her absorbed in a practical way outside the hospital. Assuming some progress with Wilfred he wanted him to be looking forward to a change, a new interest: Wilfred did not realise it yet but a medical career was out of the question. As Eileen had to see Mr Jenkins about the mattress he took the opportunity:

'Mrs Willett, do you have any plans when your husband is better?'

'Better, oh good, you do believe that, don't you? I do. Well, we'll have to find a home. I've thought about it a bit but I wanted him well first.'

'I think it would be a splendid idea to start looking now. Where do you think?'

'My father-in-law thinks Kent is a good idea and did mention something about a friend keeping an eye open for a sound buy. But of course we can't afford too much and will need help from our parents, which will make it difficult.'

'I can imagine that. But you get on with it and I'll put Wilfred right. He's far too brilliant for us to let anything happen to him.'

'I'm bound to be in trouble with Wilfred's mother when it comes to our place. She hasn't forgiven me for marrying him.'

'I'll support you,' he said, spreading his hands and smiling. He seemed so sure of his direction, no wonder Wilfred took strength and inspiration from him when he was studying there; no wonder he was more hopeful now.

Five days later, the day before Mr Jenkins was due to operate, Eileen spoke to Wilfred, her eyes full of news.

'You're looking better, honestly, everyone says so. Mrs Thumper noticed a big improvement and Mr Jenkins is very hopeful. Do you know what he said to Mrs T? He said, "Oh, he's far too brilliant, Mrs Willett, for us to let anything happen to him. We'll need his help here again when he's recovered." She was so proud, so proud.'

Wilfred's hand went out to the chalk.

'Thank him.'

'Of course I will. Wilfred, I want to tell you something. Give me your hand, come on. Now look, you've made my dreary life worth living, you've got me out of a rich and silly rut and made me think. If nothing else I do that now. I'll never be clever or able to understand all those books to do with medicine but at least I think I'm aware of what's going on, and I'm so pleased about it. You've just got to get better. I've met you and we're married and we're going to go on. I'm lucky, Wilfred, aren't I? Because you're right in thinking that being interested is what matters most. We can't all be brilliant like you but we can try to be intelligent. And the way you say it is encouraging. Other people would make it sound an insult.'

Wilfred mumbled.

'I don't care if you don't believe it. It's true and for once you can't answer back. So you might as well lie back and listen; I'm not going to be brushed off. I'm taking advantage of you.'

Grasping the slate he wrote, 'I love you', and one side of his face lifted.

'Oh, and there is one big piece of news. Well, it isn't absolutely definite yet. It's a lovely home near Tunbridge Wells. I think we can get it and I'm going to look after you there. I've got some details but not much except that it's beautiful. My stepfather is being very helpful and we might be able to move in a few weeks. Your parents are showing an interest too. I'll tell you more about it when things have developed a bit.'

Wilfred's left hand gripped her firmly, his eyes shining. Eileen leant over to kiss him.

From this moment on she never doubted the idea: the house in Matfield it would be, come what may, and tomorrow she would write to Mrs Thumper and ask if the Willetts would like to visit the place for a day in the near future.

On her way out she met Mr Jenkins. He looked tired but was cheerfully matter-of-fact:

'Tomorrow it is, my dear, and we're all looking forward to it. Hand-picked team, best in the business, wouldn't want a better lot myself.'

'I was working it out today, doctor; it's three months and two days since he was wounded. It's taken too long, hasn't it, to find the problem. If only I could have got to you sooner.'

'Nonsense. You've done well to arrange things this far. The rest is our problem. Now you go home to your mother and arrange the curtains for the new place.'

'But I can't think of curtains tonight. Please don't say that kind of thing to me. And why can't I see him? Will you telephone me tomorrow?'

He looked at his watch.

'While you're here, Mrs Willett, could you come into my rooms for just a moment?'

'Of course.'

'Your husband, do sit down, your husband has asked me to explain one or two things to you. You can imagine the shock to his system from this injury, which has also brought on neurasthenia. His whole set-up is badly shaken, especially his feelings. He doesn't feel normal inside, you understand, he is worried that you will not know. He feels you should. I've told him not to be a silly fool and that you're a marvellous girl and I know with your tact and sensitivity he'll recover all that in due course.'

'I had guessed something of the sort. He seemed so hurt when I kissed him tonight.'

'That's the sort of problem. Your husband's nervous system is in deep fatigue, and one result is the loss of weight, a natural development, and the other thing. It's very distressing for him, I know, but fortunately he has you and if he can keep on looking forward – the house and things – he will fight to achieve something new. He's not the kind to give up, is he? We'll see what we can do tomorrow.'

* * *

Mrs Stenhouse and Victoria sat by the fire, keeping the conversation going. Lying on the chaise-longue Eileen looked at the ceiling. The afternoon light was fading.

'It *would* be a good idea to look over the house as soon as possible. I think your plan, my dear, of going down with the Willetts is just the thing. They'll obviously want to be in on it.'

Eileen did not answer. Was he dying? Was Mr Jenkins cutting into him now?

'Don't you think so, Victoria?'

'Yes, I'd love to go down. I've always liked those lovely Kentish houses, with those white boards and tiles. What fun it'll be to rearrange the rooms as you like them. I'll come and visit you as soon as I can.'

'How big did you say the garden was, Eileen?' What? The garden?

'I'm not sure, Mama. I think they said it was long and narrow, over one hundred yards.' If he lived would he be a cripple? He loved walking.

'And there's a tennis court,' Victoria sighed. 'Beautiful afternoons playing tennis – in Kent.'

If he recovered would he be only a part of Wilfred? What would be gone? Only her body was in this room. She fumbled with the images of pain, of cutting, and blood, most of all the horror of not seeing Wilfred alive again.

Eventually the day ended. She sat up most of the long night, or lay like stone. The telephone did not ring. In that small, hot theatre Mr Jenkins deftly removed the splinters, while Wilfred inhaled the smell of soaked bandages, of disinfectants and anaesthetics, the dusty dry human smell that hospitals keep even in early spring.

And in the morning they held hands, Wilfred very still. The next day he talked a little, a little more than before, and Eileen cried. He felt words and some strength beginning to suffuse his mind and limbs. Mr Jenkins was also growing in confidence but he wanted Eileen away, if possible for a day or two, so that he could be sure Wilfred had longer rests: it was essential she did not dwell on his sexual problem, essential as few pressures as possible tensed his active brain. It would have to be, he decided, a half-truth, much though he disliked them, especially to Eileen:

'Now, you can see he is much better, he really is, Mrs Willett. Of course it's splendid, really fine for him to have you here every day, but you should go down to look over the new house. That's the next stage, you know, we want his mind on it. I've talked to Wilfred about it. Let's go along and see if he agrees. By the time you come back you'll notice quite a difference in him. He's perking up every hour. Now don't be frightened. Please don't. Things are beginning to go our way. Here we are again, Willett. I've been suggesting that your wife takes that trip to Matfield right away. She can then give you all the details, can't she? Get your jobs lined up for you.'

Wilfred seemed pleased with the idea, encouraging Eileen, tapping his hand on the bed in support. 'Yes, please go.'

'Have a close look at the study for me,' he said. 'And the garden.'

'Of course I will. *Shall* I go, darling? All right, but I'll be back as soon as I can.'

CHAPTER SIX

THE ROSERY

○ ○ ○ ○ ○ ○ ○

'Of course, my dear,' Mrs Thumper said, 'you can't go on without a maid. If you insist on living in this kind of house you must have help. You simply haven't the experience necessary to run the place properly. So I've found you a man and wife. I've seen them and told them what to do. In the next few weeks before you and Wilfred move down here they can set about things. The man is an ex-regular who has been wounded. He's a smart fellow and will look after the clothes and valet you. The wife's a nice homely little woman who will be a real asset.'

Eileen was too astonished to reply, it was exactly how it shouldn't be. There would be terrible tension.

'And she's also a good plain cook. Their name is Jarman, local family.'

'But we can't afford it.'

'Don't be silly, my dear, they'll be no more expensive than paying out bits in odd labour. Mr Willett and I have been through all this. Jarman will do the garden as well, there's no knowing how long it'll be before Wilfred can do much there.

If you'll give the woman a little help in the house you'll be quite all right.'

As they'd driven through the villages Eileen had felt truly happy, welcomed by the collection of cottages on the outskirts. She loved the names on the shops: Playfair, Jarman, Lavender, Harman, Argent, Randall, Rolls, the harness-maker, the carpenter, each tiny shop with the name painted on the woodwork. She was delighted when they stopped at the coal-yard and ordered some at a remarkably cheap price. She *could* manage! It was as they passed the massive square tower of the church, with the high-walled rectory, that Mr Willett mentioned, by the way, they had, in fact, been down a few days before to arrange things at The Rosery. Very upset, Eileen said she was grateful for, as he put it, 'the hand'.

Low ceilings and a central wooden staircase made the house warm with atmosphere. It would be good to live there! Eileen looked across the study – outside, a row of pines climbed up the slope, and the south wall was shielded by a magnificent pear tree. Mrs Thumper, meanwhile, was inspecting the drawing room, moving the french windows back and forward on their hinges. They were not quite right. The oasthouse over the lane took Eileen's gaze through the apple orchard: Wilfred could make his way across the orchard, taking his time, coming back to his chair. And she would read to him.

'I'll have a good look at the kitchen and scullery,' Mrs Thumper said. 'Rats can be a problem in the country.'

Eileen slipped out into the garden, chill in the March light, looking with eyes for Wilfred. The damp, thick grass on the tennis court bleached her shoes. Passing beyond the square vegetable patch she brushed her sleeve against some bushes and turned to look across the court, on which dim marks of summer lines still lay, past the stables to The Rosery. Mr Willett was coming out of the house. Eileen ducked under a low branch and hurried towards a hut just visible at the far end of the garden. This whole area was patterned with crocuses, bluebells and double daffodils.

She pushed open the door, jammed with swollen wood. She managed to see round it. *This* was the place for Wilfred! The study in the house would do for everyday, but here, especially in summer, he could think and work and write. Beyond the hut there was a clear view. The country was flat, long and low, sweeping until it rose into heath and the green downs. In this ordered, natural setting she had everything she needed to help Wilfred back to health, everything for his new life. Mr Willett was standing beside her.

'Fine sight, isn't it, even today? And I see you've found a hideaway. My girl, you know how much we hate debt, do you think Mrs Willett and I would suggest something you can't afford? In fact I've put a bit by to see you through. We've arranged for the Jarmans to come here next Friday and they'll send you a postcard to say how things are going.'

Eileen flared.

'Oh, why can't you leave us alone – to live in our home in our own way? You didn't even want us to take this place. I don't want your beastly spies in the house, and I'm sure we can't afford them.'

'Don't take on so. We're only trying to help. Mrs Willett's

an awfully good manager, you know, very economical. I know we've made lots of mistakes in the past – don't know how much it's grieved me – and we want to take care of things while Wilfred recovers. Proper staff help, you know.'

'What do you know about expense when she spends sixty pounds a month in food and maids' wages?'

How did she know that? Mr Willett was astonished at this accurate detail but he assumed an air of gentle forbearance. She was going through a very trying time and he wanted to avoid more bickering.

Now where could they put the chickens? Eileen knew Wilfred wanted to keep some. And she must buy some back numbers of *The Smallholder* because he'd enjoyed rummaging through one which had been left lying around at the hospital. Eileen faced Mr Willett.

'If we got some chickens where would we house them?'

'You'd better ask Jarman the best way. Sort of thing he'd enjoy.'

They walked together across the grass back to the house. Mrs Thumper was coming downstairs.

'It may be a little dull and dour here for a while but people *will* call in time. It's quite a decent house. Five bedrooms should be plenty, even giving one up to the Jarmans. They're on the small side but never mind. There *is* a shortage of bookcases, my dear, and Wilfred does love to have his books around him.'

'I know. I'm looking forward to reading to him.'

There was a knock on the door. A youngish woman stood there pointing over her shoulder.

'You wanted to see the cob, sir.'

'Mr Fuller, isn't it?'

'Yes sir, he's in the road with her.'

Mr Willett followed the girl down the path, Eileen behind him. What was he up to now?

'Like the look of this one?' A heavily built man with a fat, kindly face was sitting in a dog-cart, with a beautiful chestnut in the shafts. The brass on the harness shone.

'I do. She looks a fine animal.'

'That she is. Never had a finer,' Mr Fuller replied. He looked like a retired shopkeeper, none too careful of his appearance, with a shabby dark coat and trousers. Eileen noticed there was no arm in his right sleeve and he carried no whip in his left hand. She moved nearer the horse and smiled up at the man.

'Yes,' he went on, 'and I break my own horses and no one has anything to do with them but me. Would you like to try her? Can you get up into the cart, do you think? Come on, Maggie, will you give a help to the lady?'

'Are you sure you are all right, my dear? You are not going to drive are you?' Mr Willett was concerned.

'Yes, I am all right, don't worry.'

'Julie's as safe as houses, sir, won't risk anything untoward, I can tell you.'

Eileen drove off, her hand trembling with the thought that she might catch the gatepost or allow the trap to be upset. But Julie was delightful to drive, her mouth responding to the softest guidance. They trotted away between the cold hedgerows, past the cottages towards the quiet, brown village.

'And I must never use a whip?' Eileen asked.

'No, a horse that wants driving with a whip is no good to me so I break 'em without. She's just the job for you. And your husband, miss. Hey, look at those spinks over there! Nice and early this year.'

'Spinks?'

'Well, chaffinches you'd call 'em. Spinks is the call they make.'

'I must tell my husband that.'

They trotted around the village green. The dark pond was brightened by one swan trimming slowly after another.

'What's that house?'

'Matfield Place. But you must see The Friars if you haven't. Fine old place, Elizabethan it is, down the drive opposite the place you're taking. Go past the apple orchard. And beyond The Friars you got the Lake.'

'How long would it take to walk from the house?'

'Maybe ten minutes, no more.'

'I'll do that when I get back.'

The postman came by on his bicycle, steadily pedalling, his wheels leaving a sharply defined track on the frosty road.

'Fine day,' he shouted up at Mr Fuller.

Eileen drew up, impressed and amused by her skill. The postman moved back a few yards in line with her.

'And fine news from the Front,' Mr Fuller replied. 'I knew they'd stick it out and not let us down. This is Mrs Willett who's taking The Rosery.'

'Oh, yes.' He smiled, and on he cycled, down the still lanes.

'If Julie really is for sale, Mr Fuller, how much do you want for her?' And off they trotted again.

'Well, let's say if you like her the gentleman says he'll settle up with me. See, I hate selling her, to be honest, but I was driving through couple of days ago and he stops me and said he liked the look of Julie. "So do I," I said. Seemed rather odd to me, then he told me about your husband, his son, being wounded and not too strong as yet up in London. So as I knew I'd be all right for another horse and he needed one a bit sharpish we fixed to see you today.'

'She's a lovely horse.'

'And I can arrange for the harness, whip and furnishings if you like. You've got a stables there I know.'

They skirted through a few small woods. Two men were standing by a pond. Excited by the cold air on her face and the thrill of the understanding horse Eileen swept round the corner and back to The Rosery, though it was only through Julie's intelligence that they missed the post.

* * *

A week after the operation, when Eileen had been back in London a day or two, Wilfred's headaches began. Although he was now finding the words he dared not tell her. He could swallow no food, even the choice jellies were making him feel sick. When she spoke to him for hours about The Rosery he breathed with extreme control and by keeping a firm grasp on the side of the bed kept a steady face.

'There's a blue tiled fireplace, and I can get a thick blue carpet, Mama has seen one. I think you'll like your study, your father says he's found some well-padded chairs – he's been so kind, Wilfred, I really do love him now. And the garden. There's the most beautiful big pear tree leaning over the house, and an orchard across the lane. We're terribly lucky with the garden, it's so big, and there's a perfect little hut for you, miles away it seems. I don't know a thing about gardens but I can look after the herbaceous border.'

Wilfred tried to concentrate between the thumps. Chairs? Carpets? How on a small income, only the wound pension, even supplemented by Father, how could they manage? Surely it was all out of control, why had they let themselves in for it?

'I should have liked to do it all myself,' Eileen went on, 'we shouldn't have been so grand, and we'd have made mistakes, but it's too late now and I mustn't have any more rows with your parents. I've been to blame in many ways, I know I have.' A nurse came in, pretending to be annoyed.

'Now, Mr Willett, it's coming up to your mealtime. You didn't eat at all last time. Well, you've got another visitor, but once he's gone you must have something.'

'Wilfred, it's Piers, Piers Bentley's come to see you. He called on us the other day.'

Piers was in uniform. Wilfred could remember the face and the puns. He stood at the end of the bed, smiling down.

'How good to see you! I heard all about you from Mrs Stenhouse when I popped in there on Thursday. Very sorry to see you've had such a rough old time; thank heavens you've landed in this place, first class I'm told.'

'Well, I'll leave you two to talk,' Eileen said.

Wilfred made a big effort: 'How are you? Where have you been?'

'Oh, fine really. I've been at the Front, like everyone else. I've got a couple of weeks' leave, spent most of the time walking along the streets, just enjoying familiar sights, and seeing some old friends. I do hope you haven't been too bad. What rotten luck!'

Wilfred decided not to reply. Piers walked to the window, leaning against the woodwork. A breath of wind rattled the top of the blind. For a few long moments there was silence and when Piers spoke he did not turn.

'Do you ever see the papers? They're full of lies, aren't they, not a shadow of truth in most of them. The journalists who send that stuff back should be shot, well, damn well told. And the editors here.'

'Yes.'

'There is not, as they claim, not the *slightest* likelihood of "an early termination of the war". I hate it, the whole damn thing, I've had enough, I'm afraid.'

He turned round.

'But tell me what happened to you? Tell me about Eileen. So it all worked out after Trinity. It's wonderful to see you married. You must have felt cock-a-hoop – at the time.'

Wilfred shook his head, waving love aside.

'Please go on.'

'What I think, d'you mean?' Piers sat on the end of Wilfred's bed, Wilfred as pale as the sheet. 'I'm not sure I can express it. When I went out I tried very hard, no finer fighter and all that. After all I hadn't exactly made much of a show at Trinity, had I? So I tried to get to know the ropes, the trenches,

160

chains of command, expectations of an officer, all that. Perhaps I'd often thirsted for that kind of thing, always hoping to come through of course. But you were unlucky, Wilfred, damn the whole set-up. It's worn me down. I grew to hate the bad language first, then it became the billets, the mud, the field kitchens, everything. Sleeping on straw, it's unspeakable. And then people get up to childish games and what they think are the most wonderful ruses – but they're only trying to escape their fear.'

Wilfred nodded Piers on. He wanted to drink it to the full. Piers's voice was now strained but stubborn, not a trace of Cambridge, all buoyancy gone.

'You probably don't approve of that, Wilfred. I've hardly ever spoken like this before. It's only because I've always respected you, no, I mustn't start that . . . And you realise we've made some damn-fool errors on the Front, not the fault of the rank and file, they only carry out the orders. I did write one letter full of my thoughts but it wasn't meant for anyone so I tore it up. Best thing. I suppose I'm simply afraid. Some of the best men, too, have gone. You probably heard about Blandford, from Trinity? You remember Montenegro? And of course David Rutland. You didn't? I thought as he knew Eileen you'd have heard. Yes, last month.'

Wilfred was shaking, his face a desolation.

'Look, I'm sorry, can I come back to see you again? I'll be more cheery then. Don't know why I've said all this. Stupid of me. I went out to dinner last night, too, and wanted a quiet time but everywhere you go some damn fool wants to talk to you. Now I'm doing the same.'

Moving towards the door, Piers suddenly moved back to Wilfred and squeezed his arm. Wilfred shut his eyes when the door closed. Oh God!

The nurse came in, carrying a tray of food.

'No, I'm sorry,' Wilfred moaned, 'I can't.'

'That's not the way, is it?' – the sister was standing behind – 'you've made up your mind before you start. A lightly boiled egg is what you need.' Wilfred did not move. What was the use of arguing? While Eileen watched he ate bread and butter, and half the egg; he looked up at her intently while she congratulated him. He vomited all over the bed. Eileen rushed out and within minutes the evening sister and Mr Jenkins were by Wilfred. Eileen was asked to leave.

Ten minutes passed. Mr Jenkins came out and took Eileen with him.

'Now, let's explain. The acute cerebral pressure is there again, curse it, and I think we've got another developing abscess. This could mean a further severe attack. I'm not doing anything until tomorrow when I'll open up the wound and insert a tube for drainage. But, believe me, we're not in a worse position than a couple of weeks ago; we must keep a close eye on him, day and night. He must be absolutely still. By the way, did you notice anything unusual today?'

'No, I was gabbling on, I'm afraid. Then Piers Bentley came in. When I got back Wilfred had a few mouthfuls, then suddenly went even whiter . . .' she sobbed.

'I think we'll have to leave him alone for a while, don't you? He mustn't make this extra effort to talk, even though he is coming on well with his words. We want him as quiet as possible. After the drainage we'll let him see you again.'

Wilfred was dozing, exhausted, his mind in slippery darkness:

'So many people, all my life, especially my mother, have told me I was doing foolish things and would suffer for it. I slept in the snow in winter before I was fifteen and spent rainy nights under hedges. And then Belgium and shell-torn poplars. David, not David! I've got away with hundreds of things, always felt fine. Now I'm frightened. It's all slipping. It's been cold for a long time; I can hear birds crying. It's raining now and the wind is cold. The wind is blowing outside, the trench is grey clay, must I go to the sap head? David, I want to walk along a cliff until it ends in a sharp drop to the sands. I've made a mess. One stupid moment, they aimed straight; puffs of smoke in the distance, no one else to blame. Thousands of men are still out there, hundreds of thousands. But you! I obeyed my best instincts, bore the brunt, all so futile. Cheap exhibitionism. David, how did it happen to you, why you? I'm clean and tidy and useless. I tried something that normal people do not attempt. Was I nerve-racked? I must go down on the sands, the sky must be clear steel, the air crisp with frost, down nearer and nearer the one-note murmur of low tide. I will stop and let the water lap over my shoes. I will stop.'

They checked him night and day, knowing nothing of his blurred turbulence. Kissing his blank face Eileen sensed his despair, the bird's cry in his mind.

'Will anyone come to help me? What was Cambridge for,

why was David so balanced, what was medicine for – no one was helped, what is the point of knowing anything, Vega's blue light, the binary stars, the nebulae and other systems? Why our desires if they're not fulfilled? If I walk into the waves will my feet carry off, for I can't swim like this, more than a stroke or two like this, will the small breakers end me? Eileen will weep, God knows, she'll see the wreck of her hopes. And there are no beautiful dead bodies, not in Ploegsteert, not in this hospital. Will Jenkins let me go?'

As the suppuration gradually involved more tissue the crisis approached. Yet, curiously, despite the physical deterioration Wilfred's mental condition sharpened and his spirit rose. His eyes stayed closed, the tube running down the neck. He had only teased the foam with his foot.

'I'll talk to her soon. The small breakers? I'll talk to Mr Jenkins. Perhaps I *can* walk through them. I'll walk. I'll take our children for walks. If I fall down they'll laugh, and I'll have made them laugh. I'll show them the first swallows of the year, down on the sands, coming off the sea – now what will they be? – whitethroats and willow wrens, and how to dig for worms, quick and sharp; fossils in the cliff, they'll see sand eels and crabs in the pools. They won't know the difference, not for a while, at least, between sanderlings and dunlins, the little waders that run out to the edge of the sea. I'll wait for their flight. I haven't made a name for myself, Jenkins has, and I won't, but I won't be despicable. I'm not giving in, not if she can get to France to bring me back. Spring will come. Dandelions will be golden on the waste land, we'll hear the larks break into the sunlight. I can write.'

Eileen was leaning over him. Three days had passed. Mr Jenkins said he must not know this.

'I heard you say "I can write." Of course you can. You can jot down everything that happens in the garden – it is such a lovely garden, too – and why not write articles for the local papers, even *The Times*? "Spinks in Kent!" for a start! You could, you'd be wonderful at that sort of thing. I expect I can tell you more about Trinity than you can. Because I've been well taught! You wait until you see The Rosery. You'll love it.'

And on she talked. Wilfred opened his eyes. He heard some of this but a word was forming in his mind, slipping away, then coming back, rolling around like a black dot in the jelly of an eye. While she was speaking he worried a few words into order, he needed Jenkins, what was the damned word, what did they call it? A vaccine, a vaccine. Where the hell is Jenkins? He pulled the slate from the side of the bed and tried various letters. Generate? Jenkins would get it right.

'Please get *him*,' he said to Eileen, puffing out his lips. He had it: 'Try autogene vac,' he scraped, sweating.

'Autogenous vaccine? Willett, it's an idea, it is an idea. Don't move too much, we don't want the tube out of you. Keep still if you can.'

'I do wish he'd eat,' the nurse said.

'Do be quiet, woman!' Mr Jenkins snapped. 'I'll try to find the best bacteriologist I can to see what he thinks. We're on to something, you know, but we'll need a lot of co-operation on this one. I wonder if we can get a good man to come up with the right culture. The right culture might do it. A word with you, Mrs Willett, before I go.'

They stood in the corridor.

'This could take a couple of days to arrange. He's exhausted, of course, but mentally he's now very alert, as you can see, so it's essential to keep stimulating his interests. I've heard about the garden and birds. Good. The sister told me you've set him off on that again, splendid, and I remember he was first class in botany. Don't let him have *too* much time to think and wait for the bacteriologist. He'll fret whatever we do, but it all helps. But, I'm sorry to say this, you do understand, don't you, that although we have a chance of success it's most unlikely he'll walk exactly as he wants to – or be able to use that right arm?'

* * *

'Don't pretend you know the name of every bird just because you know a wagtail. What are the main differences between a sparrowhawk and a kestrel?'

But Wilfred's smugness cheered Eileen. She flicked through a book of coloured plates propped in front of him: his words were returning in sequences and since the vaccine inspiration he was becoming quite lively. Secretly he was also memorising wild flowers and he planned to work in a test, casually of course, on them, too. When he'd had enough of running through the names and page numbers or when his head ached he flexed his left arm muscles one hundred times. He would make it twice as strong as before. The physical effort passed the minutes and when his mind lurched back to vaccine he forced his memory forward from moorhen to heron to gull, from plate to plate, through the birds of the coast, downs, meadows, lanes and gardens, their plumage and location, even their Latin names. But, dammit, it would go to the function of the cortex, the possibilities of electric stimuli, ligatures, frogs. Frogs? Blank out and start again.

Common gull, kingfisher, heron. Heron? A heron has a long sharp bill and long legs. You see a heron flying high above the water, his great rounded wings flapping slowly. Water voles, mice, birds and their eggs are eaten by heron. And fish. Obviously. Eggs. How does the female produce? The egg becomes coated with albumen in the passage called the oviduct, and with the porous chalky shell. At last having travelled down the oviduct into the cloaca, it is laid out blunt end first in the nest.

'Willett, good to see you at it. Just to say we'll try tomorrow, and see if we can get up a resistance with your idea.'

When the big operations were finished, his was after all a simple matter in comparison, Wilfred was taken up. It was late in the afternoon. Under Mr Jenkins's precise supervision the first injection was made, and then there was only waiting.

Little happened for two days. On the third the discharge had become largely serous. Within a fortnight the wound should be finally healed, Mr Jenkins assured Eileen, but there were many more lasting problems:

'The paralysis down that side, too much happened in those first weeks after he was shot, I'm afraid. There will be some movement in a couple of months, possibly quicker when he's happily settled down in Kent and itching to be about the place. All rather vague, I know, I wish I could be more certain.'

Before long Wilfred was strong enough to lever himself up on his bed, lean over a chair and see the Zeppelins tilting up in the sky. Once, flames burst from a building opposite and a nurse hustled him properly into bed.

'You really should not be doing that. I thought you had more sense. Mr Jenkins is on his way to see you.' He clearly could not stay long.

'I'm afraid I won't be able to see you again. The hospital is full, people are standing in the corridors waiting for attention. Masses to do, and anyway you're on the mend. I should think you'll be away from here in a week or ten days. Incredible sight outside, isn't it? Over London. When I think of all the talk when one's young about right and wrong, rules of conduct, the educated man and so forth. All that hasn't helped much, has it?'

'I don't know,' Wilfred replied, 'I don't know. The nurse told me there are a lot of casualties from those things.'

'There are.' Mr Jenkins sat down. 'I was walking home, the night before last I think, and there was a huge fellow lying on the pavement. I nearly fell over him. No more than a hundred yards from here. He must have crawled some of the way. I raced back for a stretcher and to get some help. The chap, he looked like a docker, enormous size, said, "Give us a cig, doctor. Mine got blowed out of me pocket." I gave him one and lit it for him, then asked him where he was hit. I felt for his pulse but couldn't find it except faintly in his neck. He said, "Legs, I think, doc, but they don't hurt." I pulled the blanket off his legs. They were literally hanging on by the skin, vagus nerves, anterior triangle, done for. Why he hadn't bled to death I don't know. I couldn't do anything but order him to be got ready for the theatre, and to pump caffeine and morphia into him. In the ward they couldn't even get the saline into him before he kicked it.'

'The CNS couldn't react any more?' Wilfred felt self-conscious about this obvious remark.

'You seem much livelier, good. You're full of talk, too, with the nurses, aren't you? One of them told me you're "fun to confide in". Dangerous! By the way, watch the very charming sister.'

'You don't mean Madonna?'

Wilfred had talked a little to her, an almost angelic person, sympathetic, soft, with sallow features.

'Dreadful! Avoid her like the plague. She has a nasty spiteful temper and corrects the nurses in the hearing of the patients.'

'That's hard to believe.'

'Yes, she took me in, too. She's as hard as a bullet. Too many of them like that.' Mr Jenkins looked askance and indignant. 'Well, it has been fun having you here. I wish you'd been brought here sooner, but there we are. I'll miss you.'

'I'm not going to spend six months in a bath chair, I can tell you. No one is going to pull me up and down any Esplanade! By the way, do you know Kent, around Tunbridge Wells?'

'No, I don't, but I've heard all about it. Good luck. You'll survive!'

Halfway out he turned, he'd forgotten something.

'Oh, how's the spelling?'

'Not too bad. Punctuation still chaotic.'
'Ah, well. Come and see me when you come to London.'
'Of course I will. And thank you.'

* * *

Growing proud in strength every day, sometimes spending up to three hours leaning on the end of his bed, Wilfred did not waste his last week at the hospital. He was reading up on swifts. The nurses, on a rota system ruthlessly insisted upon by Wilfred, tested him. First he had to write the name of the bird, then enumerate the facts.

'Swifts. Oh, come on, Wilfred, they're easy.'

'Huh! Not in the same family as swallows, but near relations. You see them flying high in the air above towns as well as villages and the countryside.'

'Yes.'

'They look quite black when you see them against the sky, but when they swoop from on high right down to within a few inches of the stream' – his left hand dived – 'you will see that they are really sooty brown in colour without any white, except a little at their throats. Swifts seem to dive like this mostly in May and early June, so in fact, nurse, you must look out for them.'

'Concentrate, please.'

'You will hear the swishing sound as they hurtle by and you wonder how they can ever pull out of their dive, but they can, they don't crash, they glide up again. They cannot run about, of course, as their wings trail on the ground, and their legs are short and weak.'

'Not bad.'

'*Not bad?*'

'Marvellous. Word perfect, I'll forgive you the irrelevant additions. Now the sand martin.'

'Nurse, look, look at that Zeppelin. I can't concentrate, I'm sorry.'

'You've seen plenty of Zeppelins.'

But this one filled the window and Wilfred's mind. He thought of it all, and of them all.

'Anyway, I suppose it is time to stop. Your wife will be here soon with the car, and you'll be off. We'll miss you. Where does the train go from, Charing Cross?'

'We stop at Paddock Wood. How does that sound to you, nurse?'

'Lovely.'

Eileen found Wilfred sitting alone. Her mind dancing with happiness, crying, she was too excited to speak. She scooped up his few belongings into a small case. It really was time to go.

'But we must say goodbye to Mr Jenkins, darling, we must.'

'I've done that. He came in and we said our farewells. He's very busy now. He did send his best wishes, said he was very sorry to miss you.'

'Well, what about all the nurses?'

'No, I'll write to them. Some are off duty, anyway, and I've asked two to help me to get outside.'

Slowly Wilfred was carried, occasionally taking his own weight on the ground, to the waiting car. As the doors opened he saw three men being carried in on stretchers. The door closed out the moans from one of them.

They were away, and he leant back. Well, he could not yet walk for two paces without falling headlong, he could not spell accurately, and he might not be able to talk for five minutes without making silly mistakes or feeling giddy. And it did look as if there would be no more strolling around galleries or lying in the ferns. That was another world. Yet he was going to live, and to live with Eileen.

'And I'll write,' he muttered.

'Yes, darling.'

He looked at Eileen.

He would go on finding out everything about ornithology, learning about birds by watching them whenever he could. And he would keep a diary of everything he saw in the garden at The Rosery – and in that orchard and on that lake. If he couldn't sleep he'd get up early to study, really study. He'd be scientific in his approach, none of this dabbling. When he could write better with his left hand he'd go up to the hut at the end of the garden and put it all down. The car made its way to Charing Cross. Yes, that's what he would do, he'd keep a diary.

TWO ENTRIES FROM
WILFRED'S DIARY

○ ○ ○ ○ ○ ○ ○

1919   October 15th. Marjorie Audrey born. Plant apple tree
        in orchard.
1923   May 6th. Anne Eileen born at The Rosery.
        Flycatcher seen.

AFTERWORD

○ ○ ○ ○ ○ ○ ○

In a sense, two of my novels – *Wilfred and Eileen* (1976) and *Summer in February* (1995) – were 'given' to me. Both those books came directly from conversations I had as an English teacher at Tonbridge School, one with a pupil, one with a colleague. Both are what is loosely called 'true stories', and both are set in 1913 and 1914.

I came across the lives of Wilfred Willett (1890–1961) and Eileen née Stenhouse (1892–1961) in a rather roundabout fashion. In the early 1970s I was hoping to write something on Siegfried Sassoon, either a biography or a critical introduction of some kind. And I intended concentrating not so much on Sassoon's war poetry, which was already widely known if not becoming obligatory in the classroom, but more on his undervalued prose and in particular on the semi-autobiographical *Complete Memoirs of George Sherston*. I have always greatly admired that self-effacing trilogy.

The first of the three books, *Memoirs of a Fox Hunting Man*, is located in and around the Weald of Kent, where I live, and although the place names have been changed it isn't difficult to spot Tonbridge, Paddock Wood, Sevenoaks, Matfield and so on. The central character and narrator, George Sherston, is of course Sassoon's *alter ego*. The setting is an upper middle class world of farm carts and slow trains and point-to-points and village cricket. It has a nostalgic feel. The second (and most famous) volume of the trilogy, *Memoirs of an Infantry Officer*, pitchforks George Sherston and the reader from the serene innocence, if not complacence, of that country house rural England straight into the trenches. It is, of course, one of the great books of The Great War.

So, one morning, when I was teaching some poems by Isaac Rosenberg, my mind was also on Sassoon's journey from the Flower Show Cricket Match to the Somme to Craiglockhart Hospital. After the lesson I found one of my pupils, a very able one, waiting for me outside my classroom door. It was Anthony Seldon, now the Master of Wellington College and an accomplished political biographer, standing there in the corridor, looking much as he does now, a sixteen-year-old.

'It's just that. . .' he said, 'it's just that something really extraordinary happened to my grandparents. Back in the First World War. I didn't want to mention it in class, but I've been thinking you might like to know.'

'I would. Tell me more.'

And he did. He told me the story of Wilfred and Eileen, only the barest of outlines, in a chat that probably lasted no more than five minutes.

Anthony explained that his mother, Marjorie Seldon, had considerable autobiographical material left by her father, Wilfred Willett, and that Marjorie had tried unsuccessfully to find a publisher. Would I like to speak to her about it all, to find out more, and perhaps to read what his grandfather had written? Yes, I would. The very next weekend I drove over to their home near Sevenoaks, where Marjorie and her husband, Arthur Seldon, the distinguished economist, lived. Two hours later, encouraged to 'see what I could do with it', I was on my way back with Wilfred's battered manuscript beside me.

On one level, it was easy enough to understand why no publisher had yet been found. Much of it read as an unremarkable philosophical tract, tracing the path of Wilfred's political beliefs, but in the early part I could see a shattering and inspiring story. Those pages of Wilfred's, I realised, had something of Siegfried Sassoon's simple directness and self-effacement, yet both men were not as simple or as self-effacing as they at first seemed. They were tough individuals. They'd had it good and they'd had it bad. Though different in so many ways, Siegfried and Wilfred were privileged and talented and trusting young men who had no inkling of what was to come. Both had been to famous public schools, Marlborough and St Paul's, and both were Cambridge graduates whose fortunate and promising lives seemed destined for the top. Then both had been traumatised by bullet wounds, after which each took up a political and moral position which set them sharply at odds with their own class.

And, of course, at the very heart of it all was a wonderful love story.

Moving on, how on earth did Wilfred ever come to accept that his career as a surgeon had been blown away? All right, he had no choice. How did he endure his lifelong disability and stay so positive and become so helpful, day in and day out, to so many others? I was moved by Wilfred's astonishing courage and idealism. As for Eileen: how on earth did she overcome every obstacle and get to France on her own and bring him back? How could a woman of her conventional background be so assertive and tenacious and strong? I was overwhelmed by her extraordinary determination. In her refusal to be beaten she was in every way the equal of Wilfred. And who could not be deeply touched by their passion, their secret marriage and their total devotion to each other?

The facts were there. It is, however, a tricky thing lifting out a section of a real person's life and trying to turn it into a novel. When writing fiction or drama about real people in the past the further back in time you go the easier it is. You can write just about anything you like about the Romans and the Elizabethans. It is much trickier if the direct descendants, the close family, are still living. A father's real life or a mother's real life is more than a 'story' to a living son or a living daughter; it's far more important and far more potentially touchy than mere historical material to be shaped and re-written.

Marjorie Seldon, the most devoted of daughters, had entrusted me, then, not only with a manuscript but, in a way, with the private and intimate lives of her parents. Whatever I wrote, if it were published, would establish how Wilfred and Eileen were – from then on – to be known and to be remembered. From the first moment I started writing the book Marjorie was a massive help, open-hearted and open-minded, and in her own approach as determined as her parents in seeing something through. She backed me and she trusted me and she said so.

Yet this always felt delicate territory. I was planning to transform a small part of a largely factual manuscript into a novel, and in this I knew I had to tread very carefully. While trying to make the story 'work', I needed to think hard about the issues of freedom and licence. I would have to use my imagination, you can't write a novel if you don't, but I should be wary of taking liberties. Where exactly should I play straight, and where could I reasonably embellish?

When you research a historical novel you spend months, years even, reading, taking notes, going to libraries, interviewing people, looking at old photographs and poring over diaries, revisiting places and taking new photographs. Then there are the quiet hours of sitting and waiting and staring and feeling: of being imaginatively with them. You can't get away with doing one or the other. Both approaches are essential. In my determination to 'get things right' I have travelled in a planned and purposeful spirit to many places, at home and abroad, but I also allow myself the time and space to wander, emotionally and physically, and that has often been rewarded.

My first (and easiest) *Wilfred and Eileen* visit was to Cambridge, which I know well. Wilfred was at Trinity College; fifty years later I was at the college next door, St John's. There was a nice moment in the Trinity Library when I held in my hand the menu for supper at the May Ball, 1913, the very meal that Wilfred and Eileen had eaten on the day they first met each other. Were undergraduates much the same then?

Were they very like me and my 1960s friends? Yes, no, yes and no, who knows.

Then I visited hospitals in London. I spoke to doctors and surgeons and medical historians. I had less luck finding the army camp in Crowborough where Wilfred trained with the London Rifle Brigade before being sent to the Front. But years later, just after dawn one misty morning, I set off from Ypres with Wilfred's grandson, Anthony Seldon, for Ploegsteert Wood, where Wilfred was shot in the head. It is difficult to be sure now of the exact spot, to be confident we were on the very same patch of ground over which he ran to help a wounded man – only to be hit himself. But we knew that we were very near it.

Wilfred and Eileen was well received in the literary pages in 1976. The novel was dramatised on Radio 4 in 1983 and then serialised on BBC TV in four parts in 1984. Eight million people watched it. Yet over the years since this, my first novel, came out I have come to see the story rather differently. When I wrote it I was in my early thirties and I identified with Wilfred, the bold young doctor who was going to change the face of medicine and become a famous consultant, the young officer to whom the men looked up, the ambitious and confident young man with the hooded eyes who had married a beautiful girl against everyone's wishes. I now see it more as Eileen's story. My mind is more with her, and not only in the war years.

It was Eileen who, from 1915 onwards, 'ran' their life together in The Rosery, their small Georgian house in Matfield, Kent, three miles from Paddock Wood (the nearest station) and five miles from Tunbridge Wells. Matfield was then a quiet village of a dozen or so large houses and several surrounding cottages; there was a village green, the Wheelwrights Arms, the Standings Cross, the Walnut Tree Inn and the Star Hotel, and a few shops (a confectioner's, three grocery stores, a baker, a post office) and a Baptist chapel. Horses drawing farm carts with loads of hay and ponies and traps were more common traffic than cars. Later a house called Hatherleigh was lived in by the Willetts' close friends the Sassoons (distant relations of the poet).

After he left hospital Wilfred 'decided to make use of the life that Eileen had saved. He taught himself to write with his left hand and found he could walk quite fast with a stick. His physical strength enabled him to do many things that others with similar disabilities would not have attempted' (p.23 of Marjorie's 1985 book about her parents, *Poppies and Roses*). 'All his sufferings, physical disabilities and grief at the casualty lists, which continued to bring news of the loss of many friends and contemporaries at school, Cambridge and London Rifle Brigade had not lessened Wilfred's Christianity nor his patriotism' (p.37). Yet he became a founding member of the Communist Party in 1920 and an organiser for the Party in 1925 and remained a committed Communist Party member for the rest of his life.

Meanwhile Eileen was happy that living in the country began to rekindle Wilfred's interest in nature. At first he lay in his bed or leaned back in his armchair watching the birds pecking at a lump of suet that Eileen tied to a long piece of string and hung on the branch of a tree near the windows.

But soon natural history became an abiding hobby and Wilfred began to work in the garden and to record his bird observations. He wrote a novel and short stories (which, alas, did not find a publisher). He bought a pony and trap in order to explore the surrounding villages.

British Birds was published, from 1936 onwards, in the form of twenty-seven pamphlets: *Rooks, Crows and Jackdaws*, followed by *Magpies and Jays*, then *Starlings, Thrushes and Blackbirds*, and so on, to cover all the birds in Britain. It was brought out as a complete work in 1948. This was the dedication:

> To the men and women who work in our fields,
> tending the crops and livestock that we may be
> fed. By their work in all weathers throughout
> the year they shape and make the countryside
> the pleasant land that is our delight. Down
> the ages their skilful hands have changed its
> appearance when the need arose, and they will
> change it in the future. The tidy fields are
> their monument and in our countryside is
> written their history.

At the same time Wilfred started to publish a series of six small books about British wild flowers: *Flowers of Meadow-Banks and Ditches*; *Woodland Flowers*; *Primroses, Cowslips, Pansies and Peas*; *Cornfield Flowers*; *Fragrant Flowers*; *Roses, Pinks and Bellflowers*. These came out in 1937 and a collected edition appeared in 1955. He also became a regular contributor to the Communist

Party rural journal, the *Rural Crusader & Country Standard*, as well as to the *Daily Worker*, for which he was the Nature Correspondent.

Three children were born, Denis in 1918, Marjorie in 1919 and Anne in 1923. There was not a lot of money but nevertheless there was a nanny and a maid. In the 'peaceful years' of the 1920s Eileen saw Wilfred through his depressions. And his rages: all the same, Wilfred fell out so badly with his son that Denis was barely mentioned in any family memories. (Indeed, so much so, I did not even know about him when I wrote the novel.) Later she helped him through the frustrations of his surgical boot and the irons which were intended to take some of the strain off his paralysed leg. She took visitors out to see Wilfred as he sat writing or watching birds in his hut. She drove her disabled husband everywhere in her car, everywhere he needed to go, to Maidstone and beyond, all over Kent, to this National Union of Agricultural Workers meeting, to that role in the War Pensions Welfare Service, as he pursued the political vision she did not share. She helped him to make the very best use he could of the life she had saved for him.

Throughout the 1930s Wilfred sold the *Daily Worker* on Saturdays, standing at his regular selling spot in Camden Road, Tunbridge Wells. Lenin, the Revolution and Tunbridge Wells . . . Eileen was only grateful it wasn't Matfield. I can't imagine he sold many copies. Not that he would have been daunted one little bit as that left even more people to be converted. No doubt some thought him potty or a crank, mentally damaged by his war wounds. He was, in fact, an

English eccentric of a certain kind, an idealist with a hint of fanaticism.

He was also the sweetest of men. One of Wilfred's most frequent visitors in Matfield was the young Richard Cobb, later to be Professor of History at Oxford, who contributed a preface to Marjorie's 1985 book. He described going back home to Tunbridge Wells during the second half of the 1940s and the 1950s and always bicycling over to see Wilfred. He would ring up Mrs Willett ('To me, she was always Mrs Willett; she still is. It was only after Jonathan Smith's book came out that I learnt her Christian name was Eileen') and cycle through Hawkenbury and along the Kipping's Cross road, then by the primrose woods, coming out on the main Hastings road. And he would find Wilfred either in his chaotic study or the summer-house at the bottom of the garden. 'The first reward for the long ride would be Wilfred's absolutely wonderful smile, one of the warmest, most infectious I have ever seen.' The second was the tea brought in by 'Mrs Willett', 'quite one of the best, even by the demanding standards of Tunbridge Wells, the Tea Capital of the South of England in the 30s and 40s.' Richard Cobb wrote:

Wilfred radiated goodness, confidence and simple joy. He was one of the best people I have ever met. After all these years, I still miss him as much as ever, just as I can still see him, with his beautiful, slightly lop-sided smile, his rather bulbous and kindly eyes smiling too, hear his patient, halting speech and welcoming voice, and marvel at his ability to cope with his physical disadvantages.

He is still absolutely alive for me. He is one of those rare people who, just by being there, by being himself, has enriched my life and filled me with optimism about human nature.

Eileen devoted her life to Wilfred; Wilfred devoted his life to others. In the grounds of Tonbridge Castle there is a bench with a plaque which reads: 'Donated by Tonbridge Trades Council in memory of their secretary, Wilfred Willett.' When I was researching *Wilfred and Eileen* in the early 1970s I interviewed old trade unionists in the town who knew him well. Wilfred worked, they said, much harder and for much longer hours than able-bodied men. He made no concessions to his disability. 'And he was different from us. He could write really good letters.' One said to me, 'Wilfred tried to live out the Sermon on the Mount. No one has ever inspired me so much.'

I have written this Afterword in my garden hut. There are six goldfinches pecking at the niger feed outside my window. In fact, I am only a few miles from where Wilfred – in his corduroy trousers and old sports coat with leather patches – sat in his garden hut, smelling of woodsmoke, writing his weekly nature column for the *Daily Worker*. On the shelf beside me I have *British Birds*. As well as medicine, birds, flowers and politics Wilfred knew a great deal about trees, badgers and foxes. And he liked opera. So Eileen, naturally, drove him up to Sadler's Wells.

After forty-eight years of marriage, Wilfred and Eileen died within six weeks of each other in 1961. I would never have

○ ○ ○ ○ ○ ○ ○ ○

known about their extraordinary lives, let alone been able to write my first novel, without the help and encouragement of their daughter, Marjorie, and their grandson, Anthony Seldon, who waited for a word with me outside my classroom door.

Jonathan Smith,
Southborough, Kent
2013

If you have enjoyed this Persephone book why not telephone or write to us for a free copy of the Persephone Catalogue and the current Persephone Biannually? All Persephone books ordered from us cost £12 or three for £30 plus £2 postage per book.

PERSEPHONE BOOKS LTD
59 Lamb's Conduit Street
London WC1N 3NB

Telephone: 020 7242 9292
sales@persephonebooks.co.uk
www.persephonebooks.co.uk

Persephone Books publishes the following titles: